HAPPY CHRISTMAS AT FERNWOOD COTTAGES

Peggy O'Mahony

Copyright © 2025 Peggie Biessmann

All characters and events featured in this work other than those clearly in the public domain are entirely fictitious and any resemblance to any person living or dead, organisation or event, is purely coincidental.

ABOUT THE AUTHOR

Peggie Biessmann writes Romance under the name Peggy O'Mahony.

She has worked in the food, automotive and software industries and has lived in Dublin, London and Frankfurt. She is now retired and lives by the sea in Ireland.

Peggie is always delighted to hear from fans of her novels. You can contact her via her blog
http://www.peggiesweb.blogspot.com

Books by this author:

Writing as Peggie Biessmann
SPATE OF VIOLENCE
A MAN CALLED GREGOR

Writing as P.B. Barry
The Sergeant Alan Murray Series:
DEATH IN A LONELY PLACE
ENDING IN DEATH
A COLD CASE OF MURDER
THE PAST IS NEVER DEAD
THE WRONG PLACE TO DIE

Writing as Peggy O'Mahony
LOVE AT A LATER DATE
LOVE AT CLOSE RANGE
CHRISTMAS AT CASTLEDARRA
CHRISTMAS ROMANCE AT WINDFALL LODGE
CHRISTMAS AT THE WISHING WELL

CHAPTER ONE

It was raining, it was Monday and the bus was late. Millie barely managed to hang on to her umbrella in the gusting wind as she peered down the road in the hopes of catching a glimpse of the No. 316 bus. Beside her, the twins Maeve and Danny raised their voices in protest.

'Can't we stay at home, mum?' Eight-year-old Maeve's voice was shrill. 'We're going to be late again and Mrs Thomas will be cross.'

'The bus will be here in a minute.' Millie spoke with more confidence than she felt. The No. 316 bus was often late, being an extra stop on a busy route which the residents of Fernwood Cottages through years of petitioning the transport authorities had managed to have added. Even worse than the kids being late for school was the fact that she was going to be late at her cleaning job and Mrs Scott-Douglas would be cross with *her*.

'There's that new woman,' Danny observed as a car splashed past them. 'She could give us a lift.'

Millie watched the car turn the corner towards the main road. Jessica Clifford was new to Fernwood Cottages, a row of what had once been farm labourers' dwellings originally built for Fernwood House employees.

Jessica had moved into the little cottage at the end of the row a few weeks ago. Millie had seen her once or twice in Mrs

Foley's corner shop, but they had never spoken to each other. Millie had debated asking her if she needed a cleaner – she guessed from the woman's expensive clothes and snazzy car that she had money – but there was something cold, unfriendly even in the woman's demeanour. Another cleaning job, especially one so close to home would be ideal. She had talked to Mrs Foley about this the last time she was in the shop.

'I'll mention your name if she asks,' Mrs Foley said. 'But I wouldn't count on it. From what she said to me the other day, she's hoping to live closer to the city when her husband comes back. Apparently, he's abroad lecturing or something fancy like that. I gathered she doesn't like it here.'

'Then how come she moved into that little cottage? That was vacant for ages.'

'Her husband's grandfather owned it, love. The grandfather bought it off of the Hattons years ago. There's people say he won it in a game of poker with old Hatton's son, that would be the present Mr Hatton, if you'd believe that. Her husband thought it was ideal as a temporary place to live until they get a house sorted. They've been living abroad somewhere, I forget where she said.'

Millie thought about this now, standing in the rain at the bus stop with the twins getting more and more whiney as they waited. Imagine inheriting a house, she mused, imagine never having to scrimp and scrape to pay rent for an old cottage that badly needed doing up. Imagine being rich.

'Here's the bus,' Maeve said, dragging her back to the real world.

'Can you let me know in future if you're going to be late, if it's not too much trouble?' Mrs Scott-Douglas' thin lips thinned even more as she spoke. 'I'm meeting a friend this morning and

I need to get going. Can you give the bathroom a good clean? Oh, and the laundry needs doing.'

'I'm sorry. The bus was late,' Millie mumbled aware that Mrs Scott-Douglas was not even listening.

She gave a sigh of relief as her employer picked up the car keys from the hall table and headed towards the front door where she paused for a moment in the doorway, turning to look at Millie.

'By the way, can you come to me on Friday evening? I'm having a little dinner party and I need help with the serving and clearing up. I'll give you double hourly rate. About seven o'clock?'

'Yes, sure.' Millie said. She really had no option, the money was badly needed. She would have to ask Mrs Donovan to look after the twins. Mrs Donovan lived next door with her husband Podge and was always ready to pop in and keep an eye on them whenever necessary. She was a homely, gossipy woman who knew everything about everyone in the area. She refused to take any money for baby-sitting the children. 'Sure we're all neighbours, love,' she would say with a dismissive wave of her hand. The children liked her.

Mrs Scott-Douglas was waiting for an answer.

'I'll be here at seven o'clock,' Millie promised.

'Good.' Mrs Scott-Douglas gave the briefest of smiles. 'Don't be late,' she added before pulling the door shut behind her.

CHAPTER TWO

Jessica Clifford squeezed her car into a vacant space near the Greenfields Fitness Club. She liked to get here early, glad to be part of the buzz of the adjacent shopping mall. Although not much into keeping fit, attending the club gave her something to do, filling some of the empty day ahead. Today, she had arranged to meet up with Samantha (Jessica couldn't remember her last name). They had got acquainted last week at the Fitness Club and arranged to go for a coffee this morning when the Pilates class that they both attended was over.

Samantha was tall and athletic looking and during their brief conversation last week had revealed that she was into all kinds of sport. She was the mother of two teenagers and always busy. At least that was the impression that Jessica had got.

'Do you play golf?' Samantha asked later as they were drinking their lattes in the Corner Café of Greenfields shopping mall. The Corner Café was *the* place to have coffee, and they were lucky to get a table.

Jessica shook her head. 'I'm afraid not. I'm not really into sport.' This with an embarrassed smile. Samantha was already making her feel inadequate.

'Oh but you must learn. It's great fun and you'll make so many friends. Look, Alicia Scott-Douglas and I are giving a little dinner party on Friday night. Why not join us, you'd be very welcome? It would give you a chance to meet some nice people.'

Jessica murmured what she hoped was an appropriate answer, being too surprised to say no.

'You live at Fernwood Cottages don't you?' Samantha went on in that annoyingly cheerful tone. 'I always think those little cottages are so cute.'

Jessica did not think that the cottage she lived in was "cute" by any stretch of the imagination. It was small and dark and had been left in the exact same state it was in when Owen's grandfather had died last year. Jessica was currently searching for a painter and decorator although her husband Owen had advised her to wait until he came home.

'It won't kill you to hang in there for a month or two,' he'd said in response to her complaints. 'It's not worthwhile to spend a lot of money on the place until we decide what we want to do with it.'

'I didn't think we wanted to do anything with it,' Jessice had replied tartly, 'except maybe put it up for sale.'

It was all right for him, she thought, he was out in the world, mixing with interesting, educated people whereas she was stuck in a village – if you could even call it that - with a lot of old residents and a handful of people who went to work every day and were therefore invisible.

'Look,' Owen had sounded tired and even a bit depressed. 'I spent a lot of happy summers in that cottage with granny and granddad. It holds a lot of memories for me. We can discuss all this when I get home.'

'When are you getting home? You said originally that you'd be back by the end of September. We're into October now.'

'There's still a lot to be done here. I've been invited to speak at a few events in Cape Town for a week or so, which I hadn't planned on. It's important. Just hang in there, Jess. It can't be that bad.'

But it *was* that bad, she had thought in frustration as they finished their conversation. Before she moved here, she and Owen had lived in New York, in Sydney and latterly in London. They had two children, Noah and Selena. While the children were at home she had been occupied with school runs, birthday parties, sleepovers with their friends. She had been friendly with the other parents, meeting for coffee or lunch or a shopping trip. There was always something to do, something to keep her busy. She had never felt bored or lonely. Now that the children had left home – they were both studying in the UK - and with Owen being abroad, she was both lonely and bored.

Before parting, Jessica and Samantha exchanged phone numbers and Samantha gave her directions to Alicia Scott-Douglas' house ('it's only a ten-minute drive from Fernwood Cottages').

That evening as she was sipping her second gin and tonic in front of the television, Jessica began to plan an excuse to drop out at the last minute. The last thing she wanted to face was a group of married couples with no problems and beautiful homes and husbands who came home every night.

CHAPTER THREE

'Are you and Mike coming down for the weekend? It's your sister's birthday, don't forget.'

Sherry Wilson (her real name was Charlotte which she had ditched in secondary school because everyone called her Charlie which she hated) picked up on the slightly aggrieved note in her mother's voice. 'Not sure we can make it,' she said, trying to sound upbeat. 'I'll have to let you know.'

'Emma's boyfriend is coming,' her mother said, 'I wouldn't be surprised if they announce that they're engaged. Surely you can cancel whatever plans you have?'

Yes, I could, Sherry thought with a wry smile to herself but Mike can't or so he says. They had had one of their frequent rows about it two days ago. Mike had stayed over at Fernwood Cottages and she had brought up the subject of Emma's birthday.

'No can do,' Mike had said. 'It's Gerald's stag do. Didn't I tell you this already? The lads are off for a long weekend to Malaga. I won't be back until Monday night.'

'I thought you'd put the date for Emma's birthday in your diary,' Sherry said, controlling her disappointment.

He pulled a face. 'I'm sorry, love. I completely forgot.' He reached across the table and touched her hand. 'You can go on your own, surely? It's a family thing after all.'

Sherry thought of this remark now with her mother on the other end of the phone. Her younger sister Emma had only been together with Finn for eighteen months and here they were probably getting engaged and planning their wedding while she and Mike had been together for over five years with no sign of an engagement ring. They were what their friends called 'an item' but they did not live together. Mike worked in advertising on the other side of the city, where he was in the process of buying an apartment close to his place of work. He worked long hours and often travelled as part of his job and maintained that living independently of each other was the best solution.

'I don't want to spend hours in traffic trying to get over to Fernwood Cottages,' he had said more than once, 'and the same applies to you, especially with all that volunteering stuff you get up to.'

Sherry worked near the city centre as a project manager for a business consultancy. She spent a lot of her spare time raising funds for The Haven Animal Rescue, a cats and dogs home near Greenfields the local shopping centre. In fact, she spent a lot of her time working for any cause that needed a helping hand in the locality.

Sherry was not convinced by Mike's argument but since he stayed over a few times a week or she stayed with him, it wasn't worth quarrelling about, or so she always told herself.

She stifled a sigh. 'I'll let you know,' she told her mother. 'I'll be there for sure. I haven't seen Emma for yonks. What are you doing for her birthday?'

'We're having a little dinner celebration at home,' Mrs Wilson said, 'the usual family gathering. I thought it would be nicer than going to a restaurant.'

Sherry could visualise it all: her two sets of grandparents – she was blessed to have them still, she acknowledged – and her uncles and aunts and cousins. Everyone laughing and talking nineteen-to-the-dozen. A typical family get-together of people who saw each other regularly and people who saw each other a few times a year. And someone would turn to her and remark 'Pity Mike couldn't make it' and one of her aunts – usually Aunt Katie – would ask 'so when's the big day for you two?'

Sherry finished the call with her mother on the promise that she would come home on the Friday night and stay until after lunch on Sunday. Making a mental note to buy a present for her sister, she turned back to her desk and tried to concentrate on the work in hand. Her new boss Piers Halloran was a slave driver. Not only that, he was also chaotic in the way he demanded and directed what he needed. One minute it was a report on last year's turnover by client and then half an hour later he was asking her for her projections for next year's budget, expecting her to produce the figures in a matter of minutes.

'I don't get paid enough to have magical powers,' she often complained to her colleagues. 'Besides, I doubt if he knows what he wants in the first place.'

Later as she drove home, tired and irritated with her boss, her thoughts returned to Mike and his reluctance to visit her family. He had sent her a text to say he would not come over tonight as he was working very late. She was relieved in a way as she was bone-tired. Now she could dig something for supper out of the freezer and curl up on the sofa or better still, if her neighbour Zac was at home, they could concoct something together – but a little niggly voice at the back of her mind kept asking her if Mike was seeing someone else on the sly. He had a busy job, played rugby for his local club and had a host of friends, both male and female, who he met up with regularly. Was that all as easy to explain as it seemed or was she being naïve? But surely I'd notice if he had another woman, she thought.

CHAPTER FOUR

'Have you heard about the Big House?' Mrs Foley asked. The Hatton family home on Fernwood Estate to which Fernwood Cottages belonged was usually referred to as The Big House, despite the family's many attempts to call it Fernwood House.

Millie, who was on her way home from cleaning Alicia Scott-Douglas' house, looked up from counting out the euros to pay for the bag of groceries for her elderly neighbour Jimmy Daly or Mad Bobby, as he was known. He had acquired the nickname from no one knew where. She liked to keep an eye on him and his drinking pal Jimbo and usually did their shopping and sometimes their cooking for them.

'The Big House? No, I haven't heard anything.'

'Well,' Mrs Foley dropped the money into the till and closed it, then folded her arms comfortably across her bosom, preparing for a long gossip. 'You know that it's been up for sale for ages? Well, I believe it's been sold now. A businessman has bought it for half nothing, if you'll believe me. From what I hear, he's planning on making a hotel out of it. The builders were up having a look this morning and they came in here to see if I sell hot drinks and sandwiches for their lunch. Poor lads, I had to tell them I don't do anything like that.'

'I suppose that it's nice to have the place opened up again,' Millie said, doubtfully.

'There'll be big changes.' Mrs. Foley nodded her head. 'From what those fellows told me this morning, all the cottages will be converted into holiday homes. The Cliffords own that one cottage that Jessica is living in, so I suppose they'll sell that to the new owners. That'll affect you, love, won't it? I think your cottage belonged to the Big House people?'

'Yes, that's right.' Millie struggled to process this information.

Despite its defects, she loved her little cottage with its two bedrooms, small bathroom and kitchen cum living room which had an open fire. There was a small garden at the front and a paved back yard. The boiler sometimes gave trouble and she was saving hard to replace it. Her tenancy agreement stipulated that she would pay for reasonable maintenance in exchange for a low rent. The term "reasonable maintenance" had never been set out in detail and the estate agent had told her she must bear the cost of a new boiler. Her rent was considerably lower than average, for which she was grateful. She had got to know all of her neighbours, some of whom like Mrs Foley had been living there for most of their lives, and she was fond of them all. She hoped that Mrs Foley had got her information wrong and that the cottages would not be sold.

Losing access to the Big House would be a blow, too. The wide iron gates leading to the avenue which in turn led to the Big House were hanging on their hinges and she had always had free access to a little wooded area just inside the gates. In the summer, she liked to settle herself on a fallen tree trunk and get out her sketchpad while the children paddled in the nearby stream. They had enjoyed many a picnic there.

She turned troubled eyes to Mrs Foley. 'Do you really think the new owners will turn us out? Were the workmen sure that that is the plan?'

'There's going to be changes, that's for sure.' Mrs. Foley said. 'Whoever bought the place is my landlord, too. Who knows if he'll want to keep the shop open?'

Mrs Foley's little shop occupied a small piece of land a few metres from the tall iron gates leading to the entrance to the Fernwood estate. It had been in the Foley family for generations and was a blessing to the neighbourhood because if you forgot to get milk or bread or whatever, you could always knock on Mrs Foley's door after closing time and she would cheerfully serve whatever you needed.

'Oh Mrs Foley, we all need you! What would we do without the shop?' Millie wailed now. 'Some of us don't have cars and can't nip down to Greenfields shopping centre if we need something in a hurry.'

'We'll have to wait and see, love. We can only hope for the best.'

Hoping for the best was what Millie had been doing for most of her life.

Millie was brought up by her mother. Her father had been killed in a work accident when she was only two years old, so she did not remember him. She had had a happy childhood even if they were not very well off – her mother worked as a secretary for a solicitors' practice. Millie had only started university when her mother became ill and she had opted out of her studies and stayed at home to nurse her until she succumbed to the cancer which was devouring her body. It was at this point that Millie met Kevin McKenzie who was a friend of a friend. He had a good job, managing a busy supermarket. He was a few years older than her and offered security and stability when she was faced with surrendering the council house which had been her home. Perhaps that was why she had fallen for him so quickly. He was goodlooking but more importantly he seemed caring, or so she had thought. It had taken a few years before she recognised that the caring was really controlling behaviour. He had insisted that she move in with him upon her mother's death, although they had been dating less than six months. Kevin wanted children and discouraged her from returning to university. Slowly but surely he had eroded her confidence in herself. She had hoped that when Danny and Maeve were born, Kevin would be less critical of her, would love the children as much as she did. But there she was mistaken. Nothing any of them did was right.

It had taken all her courage to leave Kevin five years ago and take the children with her. Her secret frantic searches for accommodation had resulted in finding No. 2 Fernwood Cottages and the happiest day of her life since she met Kevin was when she moved in. For the first few years he had paid maintenance for the children but then he had taken a job abroad somewhere, had left without giving an address and the payments stopped, forcing her to take up any work she could find. Up until now they had managed, but if she had to find another place to live, with rents being sky high, she did not know what she would do.

CHAPTER FIVE

'I expect you're looking forward to himself coming home?' Jessica's next door neighbour Mrs Donovan looked over the hedge which separated the two cottages as Jessica walked up the path to her front door a few days later. She had been to the fitness centre – to her relief, Samantha was not there so she was spared the irritation of her company and any more talk about the upcoming dinner party at Alicia Scott-Douglas' house.

Why couldn't the old biddy mind her own business? Jessica thought crossly. She's always waiting to pounce when she sees me coming home or going out. She managed to summon up a smile.

'Yes of course.' And now leave it, she added silently.

Mrs Donovan had no intention of leaving it. Jessica was too important a source of gossip among her neighbours. 'Thinks she's the queen,' she had said with a sniff. 'No sign of the husband, mind you. Wouldn't surprise me if they were separated or even if she's married to him in the first place.'

'He'll be home for Halloween, I think you said?' She persisted now, her sharp eyes on Jessica's face., trying to detect an untruth or a shaky excuse.

Jessica gritted her teeth, she would have so liked to tell this nosy woman where to go, questions and all. Instead, she forced another smile. 'He might not be able to make Halloween but he'll definitely be here for Christmas.'

Mrs Donovan nodded, eyes snapping with curiosity. 'That's a shame. I think you said he's out foreign, Africa or somewhere?'

Jessica resisted the temptation to say "somewhere". As far as she knew, Mrs Donovan had never been much further than the centre of Dublin, if that. 'Yes, he's in South Africa just now,' she said. 'He's giving a series of lectures around the continent and that takes time.'

She turned and inserted the key in her front door, signalling that the conversation was over.

But Mrs Donovan was not finished. 'I suppose you're going to this dinner party that Alicia Scott-Douglas is having on Friday? I believe it's going to be a very grand affair. I heard her talking about it at Mrs Foley's.'

'Yes, I am.' Jessica spoke with more conviction than she felt. She still had not thought up a good excuse for not going.

'Glad to hear that. Himself was saying the other day that you must be lonely. We see your light on very late at night.'

'I stay up late reading sometimes.' Jessica hoped she sounded convincing. 'I'm not lonely, believe me,' she said, adding 'see you,' before stepping into the tiny kitchen and closing the door behind her. Her heart was thumping. What did that remark about seeing her light on mean exactly?

She slung her sports bag onto a kitchen chair, took off her jacket and hung it up on the hook inside the kitchen door, feeling relieved to be away from Mrs Donovan's scrutiny. She went to the cupboard under the sink and took out the bottle of gin which she kept there, hidden at the back. She poured herself a very small measure and drank it neat in two gulps, feeling the kick as it went down. I needed that, she told herself.

Later that evening as she was curled up on the sofa in her pyjamas, sipping her third glass of gin and tonic, she came to a decision. She would go to Alicia Scott-Douglas' dinner party just to prove to nosy Mrs Donovan that her social life was perfectly fine, thank you very much.

CHAPTER SIX

'You must be delighted that your sister is getting engaged,' Sherry's friend Zac said as he placed a steaming mug of coffee in front of her. She had popped in to see him on her way home this evening, he lived directly across from her cottage, and they had decided to cook dinner together later on. 'I know how worried you were about her when she broke up with the other boyfriend.'

'That was a bad time for Emma. Of course I'm delighted for her. Finn seems like a really nice person.' She tried to sound enthusiastic, although she knew he would see through her pretence. 'I just have a lot on my plate right now. I was half planning to work over the weekend. Piers dumped a project on my desk two days ago and I still haven't finished the SilverRing one.'

'Let yourself be spoiled. You're always rushing around. Slow down, be you for once.'

Zac was a free spirit or so Sherry was always telling him. He had lived with his grandmother at Fernwood Cottages all his life, his parents having both died in a car accident when he was a baby. He had grown up wild, mixed with the wrong crowd and no one thought he would get his life turned around but that is precisely what he did. Having always been interested in plants and flowers, he started work for a landscaping company through the intercession of a neighbour at Fernwood Cottages, Lady Moll, or to give her her proper name Anastasia Granger. He also worked for a building company, improving his DIY skills at the same time. His grandmother had died some years previously and nowadays he worked mostly as a gardener as well as doing various repair jobs around the neighbourhood. He was a familiar figure in the area, usually accompanied by his two rescue greyhounds which he had adopted through The Haven Cat and Dog Rescue. At weekends he played guitar in a band called The Wallows. Sherry sometimes teased him about his laid-back attitude and lack of a full-time permanent job.

'I get by,' he always said. 'I don't belong to anybody.'

She knew that sometimes money was tight but he never complained.

'It will be fun to catch up with everyone,' she said now, forcing another bright smile, and banishing the row she had had with Mike this morning to the back of her mind – he had informed her over breakfast that he would be away longer than planned, his friends having decided they would extend the stag weekend into a full week.

'You're not too busy for that, but when I want something, you can't find the time to fit it in,' she had said bitterly.

'We're not Siamese twins,' he'd replied in that steady, reasonable tone which inferred that she was being awkward again. 'I never complain when you want a night out with the girls. Or when you're working late or off on one of your charity campaigns.'

Sherry made no answer, although she could have said that nights out with her friends were becoming less and less frequent. Her three closest friends Lara, Bettina and Liz were all married. Lara and Bettina had small children and juggled jobs with childcare. Liz was pregnant with her first child.

As for campaigns, Sherry had been successful in helping save an ancient oak tree in the neighbourhood from being felled, and had petitioned long and hard for a local bus which resulted in the No. 316 now stopping around the corner from Fernwood Cottages. She helped to find homes for abandoned cats or dogs for The Haven Animal Rescue in addition to raising much needed funds for them.

'I'll probably get loads of hints from the family about when Mike and myself are going to follow suit,' she said now with a grimace.

Zac reached across the table and patted her arm. 'Don't let it faze you. Your private life is your private life.'

'Unless you're my family, then you practically have to explain why you're not toe-ing the family line.'

'You're going to be on your own? Mike definitely isn't coming?'

'One of his friends is getting married and he's been invited to the stag do and they've decided to keep it all going for at least a week.' This time she could not keep the disappointment out of her voice. 'He won't be back until Friday night.'

'Like me to come with you?'

Sherry hesitated then shook her head. 'Maybe no. Everyone would think you're my new boyfriend and I'd be blue in the face from explaining.'

'Whatever you think. I'm sure you'll be fine.'

She had the impression that he she had hurt his feelings by her answer which surprised her. He must know that she would have taken him up on his offer if she thought it the best thing to do. They knew each other well enough for that.

Later, she popped into Mrs Foley's shop to buy the ingredients for tonight's dinner with Zac.

'I suppose you heard the news about the Big House being sold?' Mrs Foley said. 'They're going to convert it into a hotel and I believe the tenants in the cottages will be turfed out because they want to make holiday homes of them or something.' Mrs Foley had been telling her customers this piece of news all day and by now nearly everyone at Fernwood Cottages and environs had heard it.

'The Big House has been sold? Really? I knew that old Mr Hatton died some time ago. Any idea who has bought it?'

'I didn't hear who bought it. There were workmen taking a look at the place the other day,' Mrs Foley told her. 'They came in here looking for sandwiches and they were telling me about the plans and everything.'

'But they can't just chuck out the tenants of those cottages. They've been there for years and years, well most of them anyway.'

'People with money can do anything. I only hope they leave me here in me little shop. I can't afford anywhere else, what with the price of rented property these days.'

Sherry nodded in agreement. She loved living here at Fernwood Cottages. She had found the place while a student, the low rent being a deciding factor, and had settled in very happily.

The only welcome alternative would be to move in with Mike when he finalized the purchase of his new apartment. She still had hopes he would suggest getting together at that point. Any help with the mortgage would surely be welcome to him.

But maybe it was all just rumour and speculation. There were always plenty of both doing the rounds at Fernwood Cottages. She turned anxious eyes towards Mrs Foley. 'We really don't know who the new owners are?'

'No idea.'

'Well,' said Sherry, mentally flexing her muscles, 'we'll find out and if they're planning on evicting tenants, we'll fight them.'

CHAPTER SEVEN

Reflecting on what Mrs Foley had told her, Millie was tempted to have a look at The Big House and took the first opportunity to stroll through the open gates, this morning's cleaning job having been cancelled. She walked some way up the avenue to where she could see the solid two storey building with its wide sweep in front where no doubt carriages bearing elegant ladies and handsome gentlemen had drawn up to attend the many functions said to have taken place there in days gone by. She had not done this for a very long time, being content with sitting out in the little corner inside the main gates whenever the weather was fine enough. Now she could see the grass growing up through the gravel on the drive and part of the overgrown garden at the side. She could detect no sign of life at the house and wondered if what those men had told Mrs Foley was true. At least there had been no attempt to open the place up. Maybe the new owner would decide that it would take too much money to convert it into a hotel with holiday cottages and would simply leave it all as it had been. But that would be too good and too improbable to be true.

On the thought, a black BMW, latest model, drove into the avenue and pulled smoothly to a halt beside her. The driver's window was lowered and a man peered out at her.

'This is private land,' he said. 'May I ask you to leave?'

Millie had jumped at the sight of the car and would have apologized straight away but the man's tone of voice annoyed her.

'I know it's private land,' she said, 'but I'm not doing any harm. I just wanted to have a look at the house. I heard that it had been sold and as a near neighbour, I was curious.'

The man looked her up and down and did not seem impressed with what he saw. 'Yes, the place has been sold. And it's still private property.'

Was this the new owner? Millie in her turn now looked him full in the face. He was somewhere in his early to mid thirties, she judged, and he might have been attractive except for the scowl on his face. He had a slight accent but she had no idea what it was – not American, Australian maybe? From what she could see he was wearing a designer polo shirt. The polo shirt and BMW spoke of money, of which he must have a lot if he had bought The Big House with its extensive land.

'All right,' she said, trying not to sound as annoyed as she felt – there were other, nicer ways to make the point that she was trespassing. 'I'm going. See you around probably.'

Although I hope not, she silently added as she turned and walked back down the avenue.

'He won't be much of an asset as a neighbour,' she told Mrs Foley later when she was picking up some groceries. 'I doubt if we'll be invited to any of the Christmas balls.'

'I wouldn't have anything to wear anyway,' Mrs Foley laughed.

On the Friday night, remembering what Alicia Scott-Douglas had said about "suitable attire for serving dinner", Millie dug out a simple black dress which she had not worn in ages and tied on a floral apron over it. Of course, it would have looked more professional if she had owned a white apron, but she had never needed one. She wore jeans and sweatshirts for her normal cleaning jobs. She pulled her hair off her face and clipped it in place on the crown of her head. Surveying herself in the full-length mirror in the bathroom, she debated applying make-up but decided against it. She was the servant, not one of Mrs Scott-Douglas' posh guests.

Mrs Donovan was already seated downstairs with Maeve and Danny and was reading aloud to them. She was a great favourite with the children which made it easier for Millie to leave them for the evening.

'I shouldn't be too late,' she told Mrs Donovan as she shrugged into her coat. At least it wasn't raining. And for once, she was leaving on time and hopefully the No. 316 bus would be punctual.

'Don't worry, love, I'll be here,' Mrs Donovan assured her.

The bus was only ten minutes late, which had to be a record. But perhaps on a Saturday night people either went out in their cars or stayed happily at home. Either way, Millie was pleased with herself.

The guests had not yet arrived at Mrs Scott-Douglas' house. Millie was ushered into the kitchen and introduced to Samantha Burlington. 'Mrs Burlington has done most of the cooking', Mrs Scott-Douglas told her. 'She'll fill you in on what you have to do. Oh, there's the doorbell. Some people always come early. I bet that's Lucy and Mark.' And she hurried out of the kitchen.

'Call me Samantha,' Mrs Burlington said with a friendly smile. 'Have you done any serving before?'

Millie shook her head. 'Not really.'

'You'll be fine. Come and have a look at what we're giving our guests. I'm particularly proud of my version of tiramisu even if it doesn't taste like the Italian version.'

Millie felt herself warming to Samantha and her uncomplicated manner. She could at least talk to her. Trying to talk to Alicia Scott-Douglas was like trying to have an audience with the late Queen of England.

'It's just mushroom soup for starters and then we decided on good old-fashioned roast chicken with the usual trimmings.' Samantha smiled at Millie. 'The conversation is supposed to be the centrepiece. Although I think we need a few new faces to entertain us.' She giggled and put a finger to her lips 'don't tell anyone I said that.'

Millie wondered for a moment if Samantha was already a bit tipsy. She was so unlike Alicia Scott-Douglas, it was hard to believe they were friends. Millie had had her misgivings about the guests and how she would manage, but she was starting to feel more confident now.

'Just make sure you keep everything hot,' Samantha went on. 'There's nothing so awful as cold soup or cold potatoes.'

The kitchen was big and modern. Millie gave half a sigh for her little cottage where two people couldn't comfortably stand in front of the cooker. She had cleaned this kitchen many times and emptied the dishwasher but had never done more than that. It would be fun to live in a place like this, she thought as she set out the things she needed for the evening.

Some time later Mrs Scott-Douglas put her head round the kitchn door. 'You can serve the soup now.'

Millie could hear the buzz of conversation and the occasional laugh from the guests as she loaded up the trolley with the soup, careful not to spill any. It seemed to her that a sea of faces turned to look as she entered the dining room and conversation tailed off for a moment, but only for a moment, thankfully.

Millie set about serving the guests, mindful of the "serve from the right" instructions. Most of the guests ignored her, except for Samantha who gave her another one of her big smiles.

'Thank you,' said the last guest to be served, who was sitting on Samantha's left as she placed the bowl of soup in front of him. He looked up at her and they both did a double-take.

CHAPTER EIGHT

Jessica studied her reflection in the full-length mirror in her bedroom, twisting this way and that before taking off the black and white patterned dress and picking up the silver grey one. She stood undecided which to wear. The silver grey was very elegant and she had worn it a few times to formal dinners in London and New York with Owen. Was it too dressy for a neighbour's dinner party? The black and white dress was slightly less formal. She was not sure what to expect from Alicia Scott-Douglas' guests. Not that it mattered, she told herself for the fiftieth time that evening. She was not going to become friends with any one of them anyway. Still, she did want to look her best. They would all most likely be wearing the latest fashion and dripping in jewellery. She took another sip of gin from the glass on the dressing table and tried to come to a decision. Finally, she opted for the black and white dress, adding a gold chain which Owen had given her for her birthday last year. A quick check of the time told her she had better hurry or she would be late. She downed the rest of the gin, picked up her coat and handbag. No doubt Mrs Donovan her nosy neighbour, would take note of her leaving the house, she thought as she slipped into the driving seat of her car.

Whatever she was expecting, Jessica was not prepared for the warmth of her welcome at Alicia Scott-Douglas' house.

'It's so good of you to come,' Alicia purred, taking her arm. 'Let me introduce you to everybody.'

Alicia's husband Roger came to welcome her and then she was whisked off to do the rounds of the assembled guests. Samantha greeted her with a 'glad you could make it' and then returned to her conversation with a distinguished looking man – probably not her husband, Jessica surmised. Jessica lost track of the names and the "who's who" which Alicia recited and was relieved when her hostess was called away by another guest. She would have liked a gin and tonic, just a small one, but there was little likelihood of being offered one, she thought, looking around her at what seemed like a sea of faces. She had often been to social gatherings where she did not know many of the guests but then Owen had always been there in the background. Tonight she felt vulnerable somehow.

'You look a bit scared,' said a male voice at her elbow.

She jumped and turned to see that the man addressing her was smiling at her, the glint of admiration in his eyes. She vaguely remembered being introduced to him but could not recall his name.

'I don't really know anybody,' she confessed, 'except Samantha that is, and I barely know her to be honest.'

'And now you know me,' he said with an exaggerated bow. 'I'm Ross, Alicia's first cousin, or something like it, and she takes pity on me every so often like now because I don't currently have a partner.'

Jessica laughed, feeling a bit awkward. She was completely out of practice at flirting with strangers, that was for sure.

'Let's sit down over there.' He waved towards the leather sofa by one of the tall windows. 'You can tell me all about yourself. But first, can I get you a pre-dinner drink?'

And before she knew it, Jessica was seated beside him, a glass of gin and tonic in her hand and they were chatting happily as if they had known each other a long time. Who would have thought the evening could be so much fun?

CHAPTER NINE

Recognition dawned as Millie and the dinner guest stared at each other. He was the man who had told her she was trespassing the other day. He must be the new owner of The Big House.

'This is Millie,' Samantha said in her bubbly way. 'She looks after Alicia and I know Alicia has a high opinion of her. Millie, this is Jason DeVries, he just bought the Hatton estate.' She gave one of her loud laughs causing some of the diners to turn heads in her direction and addressed Jason with a coy expression. 'Maybe you have a job for her at the estate?'

Millie felt the blood rushing to her cheeks as Jason DeVries took a survey of her face as he had done the first time they ran into each other. And, again, he did not look particularly impressed with what he saw and merely smiled politely without making a comment.

Millie resisted the temptation to empty the bowl of soup over his head and instead managed a quick nod before escaping to the kitchen. Of course he would be invited to something like this, she told herself. As a new neighbour and obviously well-heeled, he would be considered as very important, very much part of their social scene. She had better get used to seeing him around the neighbourhood. With a sigh, she turned her attention to getting the main course ready to serve.

Everyone seemed happy with their meal. Everyone talked nineteen to the dozen. Millie knew one or two people by sight. She recognized her new neighbour, Jessica Clifford, who seemed to be getting on very well with the man sitting next to her. Was that her husband? Unlikely, Millie felt. Married couples never had so much to say to each other in public, not in her experience anyway. Besides, she had heard via Mrs Foley at the shop that Jessica's husband was overseas at present.

Dessert was next on the list. Millie was glad that her part in the dining room would soon be over. She carefully portioned Samantha's tiramisu onto the dessert plates and wheeled the trolley into the dining room. There were murmurs of appreciation as the guests received their plates.

'Oh wow!' 'Looks delicious, Samantha.' And 'Very professional'.

Samantha was all smiles, clearly revelling in the praise. This was her undoing. As Millie reached her, she rose to her feet to take a mock bow and made an exaggerated gesture with both hands, catching the plate of dessert just as Millie was in the act of putting it in front of her. The plate went flying, shattering on the floor and some of the contents landed on her neighbour, Jason DeVries. There were shrieks of dismay from the female guests around the table.

For a long moment Millie just stood there and gaped, her mind a blank.

'Get me a cloth or a serviette or something,' Jason snapped at her. He began to wipe down his trousers with his serviette.

'I'm so sorry,' Samantha wailed, looking close to tears. 'Look, let's go in the kitchen and sponge it all off.'

Millie was glad to follow her suggestion and lead the way, mindful of the murmurs of what sounded like criticism from the other guests. She guessed that she would be blamed for not being more careful, but she was used to being blamed, she reflected with an inward grimace. Kevin had blamed her for just about everything during their time together.

Alicia Scott-Douglas stood up and went to put a hand on Samantha's arm, dissuading her from following them to the kitchen. Judging by the frown on her face, she was furious that something like this should happen at her dinner party. Millie refused to meet her eye.

Millie quickly produced a sponge. Jason took a seat on one of the hard wooden chairs and without a word, took the sponge from her and began to wipe off the traces of cocoa powder, chocolate and bits of sponge which were sticking to his trouser leg. Alicia appeared a moment later, apologizing profusely but he waved her away. 'I'm fine. Don't worry. I'll be okay in a minute.'

'It won't stain, I shouldn't think,' Millie told him.

He looked at her with an expression that was colder than a winter night in Antarctica but made no reply. After a few minutes of wiping – she handed him a hand towel to finish off – he and Alicia turned and walked out of the kitchen without so much as a thank you.

'Spoiled brat,' Millie murmured to herself as she got out the dustpan and brush and hurried into the dining room to clean up the pieces of broken plate and wipe off the traces of tiramisu on the floor. The guests stopped talking and watched. Once back in the kitchen, she heaved a sigh of relief. She worried that Alicia Scott-Douglas would blame her for the mishap. It would be just like her to reduce the amount she had agreed to pay her. And Millie needed that money.

It was getting late and the guests were drinking coffee and liqueurs when Alicia came into the kitchen. Millie's heart descended to somewhere near her shoes at the sight of the woman's tight-lipped face.

'Can you stay on a bit longer? Everyone is having such a good time that I think I would like to serve up cheese and crackers and profiteroles in about half an hour or so.'

She would miss the last bus, Mille thought, but she could walk home. It would only take about twenty minutes. Mrs Donovan wouldn't mind. She never went to bed before one o'clock in the morning anyway.

'I'll pay you extra,' Alicia added, seeing her hesitate.

That settled it. She certainly could do with more money.

'Of course I'll stay.' Should she mention the little "accident" with the tiramisu? Maybe not. In her experience apologies or explanations invited 'you should have been more careful' type of comments.

'Good.' Alicia nodded briefly and then returned to her guests.

It was well after midnight when Millie finally closed the front door of the Scott-Douglas residence and set out to walk home. Judging by the talk and laughter coming from the dining room, Alicia's guests were not prepared to call it a night just yet.

To her dismay, the rain was coming down in torrents and she did not have an umbrella nor a head covering of any kind. It had been a clear, mild night when she left Fernwood Cottages. As she turned the corner of the avenue, a car slid to a halt beside her. The driver wound down the window on the passenger side.

'Need a lift?'

Millie jumped as she recognized him. It was Jason DeVries. He must have left the party without her noticing. Of all the people in all the world to offer me a lift on a wet night, she thought. She pushed her straggling wet hair out of her eyes.

'Don't just stand there,' he said in the same tone he had used earlier. 'Get in.'

'I'm all wet.' To tell the truth she would rather have walked the twenty minutes home.

'And you're getting wetter. Get in and I'll drop you off. You live somewhere near Fernwood House, I think?'

'I live in No 2 Fernwood Cottages,' she told him, noting his surprised reaction. Yes, she thought but did not say, I'm one of your tenants, one of the ones you plan on evicting if what Mrs Foley said is correct.

CHAPTER TEN

Sherry checked her phone again as she sat at her desk on the Monday morning following Emma's birthday celebrations. Mike had sent her a brief text last night but that was all. She felt a lick of anger. He could at least have asked how the party went. Emma and Finn had indeed announced their engagement and there had been a big family celebration. Sherry, while happy for her sister, had never felt so lonely in her life.

'Hi, Sherry. How was the weekend? I bet you had a fantastic time.' Vicky, one of her colleagues, stopped by her desk and broke into her gloomy thoughts.

Sherry summoned a bright smile, the smile she invariably displayed to her colleagues. 'It was wonderful. Emma and Finn got engaged. We're all so happy for them.'

Vicky pulled out a chair from the empty desk next to Sherry's. 'Engaged! That's wonderful.' Vicky was single and as far as anyone knew did not have a partner which might or might not have explained her fascination with other people's romances. 'I expect you'll be next,' she added.

'We're not in any hurry.'

'Any date for your sister's wedding?' Vicky's sharp eyes darted over Sherry's face.

'Not yet.' Sherry stifled her irritation. She knew there was speculation about when she and Mike would announce their engagement. With the exception of Vicky, nearly all her colleagues were married or in long-term relationships. Sometimes when they all sat around the conference table, she would covertly study them, searching for some clue to having a successful partnership. Like her married friends, they all looked contented, sometimes stressed if they had children, but in general contentment was what came to mind. Perhaps that contentment came from knowing you had a partner to go home to every night. Why oh why could she and Mike not have the same commitment? They had been together long enough and got on really well. Mike sometimes said this was because they did not live in each other's pockets as he put it. But I want us to be married, she often thought. I want us to have children together, to be a family.

Aware of Vicky's curious gaze, she stood up from her desk to signal the end of this conversation. 'I expect they'll get married next year. In the summer at any rate.'

The phone on her desk rang and she picked it up quickly glad of the excuse to get away from Vicky.

It was Lucy, Piers Halloran's PA on the other end. 'Can you and Vicky pop into Piers's office?'

'Sure. Do you know what it's about?' Not another lightning assignment, she hoped. She was going to stay late tonight to finish off her current work and there was still other stuff from Piers waiting for her attention. She had had to put off a meeting of donors for The Haven Cat and Dog Animal Rescue until tomorrow night. She didn't want to put it off for too long, they needed money for food for the animals and she wanted to plan a big Christmas raffle with attractive prizes.

'I have no idea,' Lucy said cheerfully. 'Only he said he wants to see both of you now.'

'We'll be right there.' She put the phone down and turned to Vicky who was still standing there. 'Piers wants us in his office immediately. Any idea what's up?'

Vicky's sharp blue eyes sparkled. 'Ooh, I think I might know.'

Vicky was always pretending to know what was going on in the Inner Circle as Sherry called it. She smiled enigmatically now and followed Sherry out of the open plan office and down the corridor to Piers Halloran's office. Piers's office was bright and cheerful and had a wonderful view of the river and the city from its windows. Lucy ushered them into the inner sanctum.

Piers rose from behind his desk to greet them. 'Ladies, please take a seat.'

They all sat down at the round table in the corner. The two girls looked expectantly at Piers who was clearly enjoying himself.

'As you know, we're expanding the business,' he told them. 'As you also know, our business in Europe has hit the ground running.' He paused dramatically, Piers-style and looked at each of them in turn. 'We are going to open an office in Paris. And we are looking for someone to help with the opening and the running of the place.' Another dramatic pause. 'I feel that one of your good selves would be very important in setting up our Paris office. You are both very efficient.'

'I'm fluent in French,' Vicky said, her eyes bright with anticipation. 'I have no problem with moving to Paris. I don't have any ties here, not any that could make it difficult at any rate.'

'Excellent.' He beamed at both girls. 'I haven't made up my mind as to who is going to run the Paris office. It's something you can both think about. I wanted to give you the opportunity of presenting a good business plan. When you've done that, we can take it from there. I'd like to see your presentations in let's say two weeks' time. The office wouldn't be getting off the ground until after Christmas.'

'It's almost too exciting to be true,' Vicky exclaimed later as they walked back to their office together. 'Imagine working in Paris!' Vicky was obviously convinced that she was going to get the job.

Sherry did not know what to think. Moving to Paris was not an option. There had been rumours in the office lately about a new branch of the business opening but she was happy as she was. Besides, what would Mike say if she took off for Paris?

CHAPTER ELEVEN

Jessica woke slowly from a deep dreamless sleep. She stretched luxuriously under the duvet, feeling happier than she had in a long while. It took her a minute or two to recognize where this new sense of wellbeing came from. Usually, she woke up to the same old routine, the same vague sense of loneliness and resentment against Owen for leaving her here on her own. And lately, more often than not, she woke up with a dull headache from a glass too many of gin and tonic the night before.

Ah yes! The dinner party last night and yes, Ross. Jessica found that she was smiling. Ross had been such fun to talk to, to flirt with even just a little bit. She hadn't been so well entertained for months. Of course, she would never see him again, she was not friendly with his cousin Alicia Scott-Douglas. It was pure luck that he had come to the dinner. Besides, she was a happily married woman, if just a teeny bit lonely.

On this thought, she pushed back the covers and climbed out of bed. She would go to the gym today, she told herself. And have lunch downtown somewhere. She padded into the little bathroom with its ugly tiles and stone cold floor. Damn! She had forgotten to switch on the boiler last night, something she usually did before going to bed. Now, there was no hot water for a shower. There had always been an electric shower in any other place she had lived in and she could not get used to having to heat up water for bathroom and kitchen. This cottage is the last straw, she thought. The sooner Owen comes home and we sort out a place to live the better.

Her mobile rang as she was having breakfast. It was her daughter Selena.

'Hi mom. Did you have a good time last night? Did you meet new neighbours?'

'Hardly that,' Jessica said with a laugh. 'If you saw my neighbours, you wouldn't ask. Most of them are as old as the cottages they live in. It was a nice dinner party. How are you, darling?'

'I'm fine. Glad you had a good time. You sound different.'

'Different?'

'Yeah. Sort of upbeat or something.'

'I don't know about that.'

'Listen, mom, the reason I'm ringing. I've been invited to go to Vienna for Christmas. My best friend here at college is going with her parents and they've asked me to come, too. The Christmas market is supposed to be out of this world. I know you'd like everyone home for Christmas but would you mind if, just this once, I wasn't there?'

'Oh.' Jessica took a moment to digest this news. She had been looking forward to a family Christmas with both children and Owen at home. 'Well, of course you must do what you think is right.'

'I hate to disappoint you and Dad.'

'Who is this best friend of yours?' Selina was always making "best friends" who later morphed into "just one of my friends". But perhaps this was a boy. Selena was only nineteen and had never had a steady boyfriend, at least as far as Jessica knew. This would be another first.

'Her name's Helen Slater. You'd like her. Her mum and dad will be there to chaperone us, in case you're worried about us painting the town red.'

'I'm not worried about that. I trust you to be sensible.' But she was worried, she thought, and yet Selena had to grow up and feel free.

'Good. Will you tell Dad? I expect you'll be talking to him today.'

Owen would not object even if he was disappointed at her absence during the holidays. He adored Selena and Noah.

'I'll talk to him, but he'll be OK with it, darling.'

'Mom, you're the greatest. I gotta go. Love you.'

'Love you, too.' Jessica said.

She sat for a few minutes, deep in thought. The children were always at home for Christmas. It was a family thing. What would it be like when they married, had families of their own? Would she and Owen be happy together when it was just the two of them? For the first time in her marriage, she gave this some serious thought. She and Owen had been married for just over a year when Noah was born and Selena had arrived two years later. They had not had much time on their own without the children. At present, they talked a good deal to each other about Selina and Noah and what their futures might look like. She loved to tell him of their successes at school or sport. That was gone now because they were both at university in Edinburgh. Noah was in his second year of studying for a degree in engineering and Selina was in her first year studying history and politics. Jessica had recently read an article about marriages that were only kept together through the children. She had never thought about her marriage with Owen, never analysed if it was a success or otherwise. Never given a thought to the idea that one day the children would be gone and they would be left with each other. Was she happy at the idea? What was making her have doubts about their compatibility?

She pushed the thoughts away with an effort. She would go and visit the children in Edinburgh, she decided. Maybe at the end of October, Halloween, she could have a long weekend with them. She'd talk to Owen about it when they had their regular telephone call later on. She was just lonely here on her own, she told herself. She needed a break to clear her head and get back to normal. Besides, it would not be really too long before Owen was back and they could go house-hunting together.

CHAPTER TWELVE

Millie carefully counted the money which Alicia Scott-Douglas had paid her for the hours she had worked last night. Despite the tiramisu incident, as she called it, Alicia had been well pleased with the success of the dinner party and consequently very generous in paying Millie for the time worked.

Millie dropped the cash into the jar which she kept at the back of her kitchen cupboard. It was almost enough to get a new boiler. On the thought, she paused for a moment. If Jason DeVries wanted to get rid of his cottage tenants, there was little point in going to the expense of purchasing new equipment. She would need the money for finding a place to live. Her cottage here was ideal, being far enough out of the city to be unattractive to city workers which kept the rent low, and ideal for her in that the houses she worked in were not too far away and could be reached on foot for the most part.

'Damn Jason DeVries,' she said aloud. There was no one to hear her, the children were at school and this morning she did not have a cleaning job to go to. 'Why did you have to buy The Big House? Why couldn't things stay as they are?'

She thought back to last night. Jason had driven her home without saying a single word to her. Which was maybe just as well. He was the most rude, unpleasant man she had ever met and she would be delighted if she never set eyes on him again.

On the thought, she felt a sudden longing to walk to her favourite little corner of the grounds. It was where she went when things got her down, when she worried that her cleaning jobs could dry up and she would be forced to work further afield, which in turn would be awkward because of the children. She liked to be at home for them when they returned from school. She couldn't expect Mrs Donovan to look after them all day without paying her, even if she agreed to do it. Childminders were expensive and hard to come by out here in the suburbs.

Although it had rained steadily all night, it was now dry with a watery sun peeking out from behind the clouds. Should she risk it? What were the chances of being seen by Jason DeVries? He had dropped her off here last night but it was highly unlikely that he lived at The Big House. The place was falling down, it hadn't been used as a dwelling for at least ten years.

Before she had time to reason with herself, she grabbed her jacket, picked up her sketch pad and set off. It took her less than five minutes to reach her favourite spot. From here, the house was out of sight around the long, curved avenue so she hoped that she could not be seen from the house, should DeVries be there today.

She perched on the fallen tree trunk – it had been sheltered from the rain by the overhanging branches of an ancient tree - and took in deep lungfuls of the air which was fragrant with the scent of wet leaves and undergrowth. The gentle murmur of the little stream was soothing. She leaned back against the tree and after a minute or two got out her sketch pad and utensils. The last time she was here she had half completed a drawing of the stream where it curved gently under the trees and wanted to add more detail.

'What are you doing here?'

Millie jumped. Her sketch pad fell off her knees onto the ground. She had not heard him approach. He must have been doing the rounds of his estate on foot.

'I'm sorry. I'm not doing any harm,' she stammered.

His dark brows came together in a frown. Somehow, he reminded her of her idea of what Heathcliff would have looked like, dark and dangerous and forbidding. He bent and picked up the sketch pad and inspected the half-finished drawing.

'You're an artist?'

'It's just a hobby.' She would have liked her answer to be sarcastic or at least witty but she knew she sounded like a scolded schoolgirl.

He looked at her for a moment before he spoke, his face not betraying what he was thinking.

'I thought I told you before that this is private property. I would appreciate it if you did not trespass. I'll be getting the entrance gates fixed in a week or so in any case.'

She nodded to show she had understood. After all it was his property and he could do what he liked with it.

'I'm sure there are plenty of other places around here where you can sit and draw.'

Millie got to her feet and took the sketch pad which he held out to her. She would have liked to have the courage to ask him what his plans for the cottages were but part of her did not want to know. Time to meet that problem when it became a reality. Besides, from her years with Kevin, she had learned to avoid confrontation.

He was watching her with that inscrutable expression which she found unnerving.

'Good day to you,' she said in as neutral a tone as she could manage.

She felt his eyes on her back as she walked slowly away.

CHAPTER THIRTEEN

For her trip downtown, Jessica chose a pair of designer jeans and a silk shirt which she topped with a warm jacket as the breeze which the weather forecaster had described as "light" was really quite penetrating. She looked at herself critically in the full-length mirror in the bedroom. She had kept her figure, although her tummy could do with being a bit flatter but for a woman with two grown-up children, she didn't look so bad. Her session at the gym this morning had made her feel invigorated. She had half hoped that Samantha would be there so that they could talk about the dinner party but she was not present today. She would have liked to find out more about Ross. He seemed to be popular, as far as she could make out, but he had devoted himself almost entirely to entertaining her at the dinner, so it was hard to know. Not that it mattered, she told herself. She had enjoyed his company but that was that. Why did he keep popping into her head?

As she was putting on her make-up in the bathroom, her mobile beeped. It was Owen.

'What are you up to, Jess?'

'I thought I'd pop into town and have lunch somewhere. Just for a change. What about you?'

'I'm driving to Johannesburg later on this afternoon. I've set up a very interesting meeting there.'

He sounded enthusiastic. But then he was always enthusiastic about his lectures on molecular biology and about the students and professors he met and their ideas.

Normally, Jessica would have been interested in hearing where he had been even if she did not even attempt to understand what he lectured about,- but today she was only half listening. She broke into his recital of his plans for a weekend in a local safari park to which he had been invited. 'I spoke to Selena this morning. She says she's not coming home for Christmas. Her best friend, or at least one of her friends, has invited her to Vienna.'

'Oh. That's nice for her.' A pause. 'We'll miss her. I'll give her a buzz later on. I hope to get to see her before I take off again.'

'What do you mean, take off? I thought you wouldn't need to be away again after Christmas?'

There was a slight hesitation before Owen spoke. 'As I've just been telling you, there is talk of my giving a few lectures in South America, Brazil and Argentina to be exact.'

'You mean you're going to leave me here in this godforsaken place for months and months? That's so unfair.'

'Jess, I'm sorry but it is my job.'

'I could go to South America with you, couldn't I?'

'That wouldn't be very practical. I'll be travelling around a lot. It was different in Europe and the USA. I didn't have to travel as much there and travelling was easier anyway. You'll be fine, Jess. Have you made friends with the neighbours yet?'

'I'm thinking of popping over to Edinburgh to visit Noah and Selena at the end of the month.'

'That's a great idea. Give them both a hug from me. Look, Jess, I have to go, I have a meeting in half an hour and I need to do some preparation.'

When they had signed off, Jessica sat down again at the dressing table in the bedroom, but she did not immediately resume applying her make-up. She was not sure that she could endure another long separation if Owen went to South America. Why could he not see that she was lonely without him, without the children too? It might have been different if they were at a local college and she could see them as often as she wanted. For the first time in her marriage, she wondered if Owen was sleeping with someone on his travels. But that was absurd, she told herself. He moved around such a lot that it would be difficult for him to do that. She picked up her mascara and began applying it. Of course, there are airlines that can fly you anywhere at weekends, so it wouldn't be impossible if that was what he wanted to do, said a small voice at the back of her head.

Why am I even thinking this? She asked herself. Owen is the happiest family man in the whole world. He loves his children. But does he love me – still love me?

CHAPTER FOURTEEN

'I might have the opportunity of going to Paris to open a new office,' Sherry told Mike as they were eating dinner at her cottage.

Mike had returned from his stag do and had come straight over to her place.

'I've missed you,' he had said, the sound of his voice causing her heart to beat faster. He would always have that effect on her, she knew.

She had cooked his favourite meal, at least one she *could* cook, – lasagne al-forno - and now they were sharing it with a bottle of red wine. He had related some amusing stories about the stag do before she began to tell him what had been occupying her since Piers Halloran had spoken to her and Vicky.

'Paris? Really? Sounds interesting.' Mike took a sip of wine. 'It would be good for your career. How do you feel about it?'

'I don't know how I feel,' she said slowly. 'I think that Vicky is confident that she'll be the one to get the job. She's forever falling over Halloran trying to show what a great employee she is.'

Mike laughed. 'That might work.'

Sherry pulled a face. 'Vicky couldn't run a rice shop in a paddy field. I can't see her setting up and managing an office in Paris.'

'Now, now, that's being bitchy.'

Sherry grinned at him. 'Call it rivalry. It sounds more professional.'

'You're fairly fluent in French, aren't you? What about her?'

'According to what she's been saying all week, she's word perfect in French. But I wouldn't bet on it.'

He took another sip of wine and regarded her over the rim of his glass. 'Supposing you're offered the job, would you consider taking it?'

She shrugged. 'I'm not sure. I'd consider it, yes of course I would.'

'What would you do with this cottage? You'll hardly want to keep it on.'

Somehow, she had hoped he would be a bit more concerned at the idea of her taking off for Paris but as usual, he was looking at the practical side of it.

'If the rumours are to be believed, the tenants will be evicted and the cottages here will be turned into holiday apartments.'

He raised an eyebrow. 'Wow. Do you think they would get away with that?'

Sherry laughed. 'Over my dead body. I mean, Mrs Foley's shop would be on their list of evictions and then there are the Donovans who've been here since Noah beached the Ark, and there's Millie and her two kids in No. 2. And Mad Bobby. I could go on.'

'You haven't heard anything, though, have you? No eviction notice or anything like that?'

'No, it's all rumour.'

He frowned for a moment, deep in thought. 'But maybe you should consider moving, anyway? This place is a bit what shall I say, out in the sticks? If you think about it, it's not really a suburb and not really a village.'

Her heart did a somersault. It seemed he was about to suggest that she move in with him. With some financial help from his parents, he had nearly completed the purchase of the two-bedroom apartment, which was located in the fashionable south side of the city. She loved living here in Fernwood Cottages but she would love even more to live with Mike in Parkside Apartments.

'I like it here,' she said cautiously, 'but I admit, it does have its downside. It would be good to live closer to the office.'

'I'm sure you'll make the right decision when the time comes. Apartments are pretty expensive but if you got a decent promotion, you could consider buying something suitable. I'm sure you've been able to save a bit considering the rent here is so cheap.'

She felt as if he had slapped her. He was clearly not interested in her moving in with him. Did he see their relationship long term as them continuing to live apart? Was marriage out of the question for him? She hoped that her disappointment did not show. Mike would not like to be rushed into anything, as she well knew. He was forever lauding their respective freedoms. She sometimes thought that his married friends envied him and he enjoyed that.

'I'll wait and see what comes of the job in Paris,' she said and then changed the subject.

CHAPTER FIFTEEN

Jessica ordered a salad for lunch at a small Italian restaurant in the city centre. She had browsed around the shops with very little enthusiasm. Her conversation with Owen and his remark about doing a series of lectures in South America occupied her too much to leave much interest in the latest fashions. She would do her Christmas shopping in Edinburgh at the end of the month when she visited the children for Halloween.

She felt lonely despite the prospect of seeing the children in a few weeks' time. The sense of euphoria produced by Alicia Scott-Douglas' dinner party and her harmless flirt with Ross had evaporated.

I really need something to occupy me, she told herself as she took stock of the other diners who all looked as if they were either on their lunch break or were meeting up socially. A job of some sort, something to get me out of the house in the mornings. But what can I do? I'm not really trained for anything.

'Would you like something to drink?' The waiter having taken her order, hovered over her.

She was driving so she shouldn't really have anything alcoholic. She could have a tiny glass of gin and tonic when she got home.

'Yes, please, a glass of Sauvignon Blanc,' she told him. One glass wouldn't hurt, especially as she was having something to eat. She'd leave before the rush hour so there wouldn't be much traffic on the way home.

She was halfway through her salad, had finished the glass of wine and was debating ordering another glass, when a voice spoke from behind her, causing her to start, and the next moment Ross pulled out the chair opposite her and sat down.

'Jessica, it really is you,' he said, giving her that big smile which she had found so attractive the other night. 'I've been sitting over there in the corner and I just spotted you. You don't mind if I share your table?'

'Of course not. Be my guest.' She knew that she was smiling, that her face had flushed with pleasure.

He signalled to the waiter indicating he had changed tables and then turned to her. 'What are you up to?'

'I'm just browsing the shops and thought I'd have lunch here. What about you? Are you on your lunch break?'

'Sort of.' He gave a short laugh. 'It's very quiet at the salon today, so I decided to catch up on all that overtime I've been working lately and pop out for lunch.'

Salon? Was he a hairdresser? She could not recall if he had told her what he did for a living and now she did not want to ask.

'Great if you can do that,' she told him.

He gave her that mischievous grin which she found so attractive. 'There are perks to being the boss, I suppose.'

The waiter brought him his order and they were both silent as they concentrated on their meal.

'Are you having dessert?' He asked, signalling to the waiter.

'Just a latte,' she told him.

He ordered lattes for both of them, then leaned back in his chair and looked at her, really looked at her as if he was taking in all her features. 'What are you doing this afternoon? Don't tell me, it's the gardening club with Samantha.'

'No, nothing like that. I don't really know Samantha that well.'

'You both go to the same gym in Greenfields, Samantha told me. And you don't live very far from her. She said something about a cute little place in Fernwood Cottages.'

So he had been asking about her. She felt the butterflies starting to flutter in her stomach. Then she pulled herself together or at least tried her best to fight the sensation.

'My husband inherited a cottage in Fernwood Cottages and as he's abroad at the minute, I'm living there until we can find a house.' There, she had signalled that she was a happily married woman and not out for a flirt, in case he thought that.

He did not seem in the least put out. 'That must be lonely for you, living on your own,' he said. 'Your children are in Scotland, I think you told me?'

'Yes, they are both studying in Edinburgh. I'm going to pop over and visit them at the end of this month.'

'Both at college? You must have been very young when you got married.'

He had a way of making her feel good about herself. He'd had the same effect on her that night at Alicia Scott-Douglas' dinner party.

'Thank you,' she said, smiling at him. 'I wasn't quite nineteen when Owen and I got married. We'd known each other from school, mind you.'

'That's cool,' he said, sounding as if he meant it. 'Edinburgh is a beautiful city. I've half a mind to come with you.'

She hastily banished the vision of the two of them strolling hand in hand around the city with an ancient castle in the background. What was happening to her? She did not know how to respond. Laugh it off was probably the best way. God, she was like a teenager with her first crush.

'What are you doing this afternoon?'

The change of subject caught her unawares. 'I've nothing planned.'

'Good,' he said. 'Because I haven't either. How about we go for a drive and have an early dinner somewhere nice?'

'Well, I don't know.' Her voice trailed off.

'Look, we're both at a loose end. You'd be doing me a favour.' He held up both hands. 'No strings attached, I promise.'

Why not? There was no harm in it, surely? Owen wouldn't object. Even as the thought crossed her mind, she knew that she would never tell her husband that she had been out for a drive with another man, especially a man she barely knew.

'All right,' she found herself saying. 'I'd like that.'

He flashed one of those heart-stopping smiles at her. 'OK, let's do it.'

CHAPTER SIXTEEN

'You haven't heard anything from your landlord yet, then?' Millie's best friend Keely asked.

They had met up at Greenfields shopping mall for a coffee. Keely lived the other side of the city so they did not get to meet very often but they kept in touch by phone on a regular basis. Keely knew all about the encounters with Jason DeVries.

Millie shook her head. 'No one has heard anything so I'm sort of hoping it's just all gossip and rumour.'

'You said Mrs Foley had met the workmen, though?'

'She did and she seems pretty sure we're all going to be served notice any day now.'

Keely fixed troubled eyes on her friend. 'What will you do if you have to leave Fernwood Cottages?'

Millie toyed with her coffee spoon. 'I really don't know,' she admitted. 'I can't afford anything even half decent. I'll never find anything again with such a reasonable rent, that much I do know.'

'Could you take on more cleaning jobs? Or maybe work in a hotel or a restaurant or something like that?'

Millie shrugged. 'Restaurants and cafes don't pay that much and the hours wouldn't suit me.' She forced a smile. 'Something will come up if I really do get evicted.'

Keely was the only one of her friends who had stayed in touch with her when she moved in with Kevin. Despite all his efforts to separate her from everyone – any time she made plans to meet up with her mates, he inevitably found a reason why she had to cancel – Keely had hung in there while the others had given up and moved on.

'What about council housing?'

'I'm not on the list. When I left Kevin and got No. 2 Fernwood Cottages at such a lovely low rent, I felt I'd be OK. I sort of planned to go to night classes when Maeve and Danny are a bit older and get a better job later on. The cleaning jobs aren't bad, you know. Money is a bit tight always but I've managed fine up to now. And I love it here. It's practically in the country. Great for the kids and the neighbours are the best.'

'I'll keep an eye out for anything round my way,' Keely promised.

Millie's mobile beeped and she checked the caller ID. It was Alicia Scott-Douglas.

'Hi Millie,' Alicia said in her brisk no-nonsense way, 'could you come over to me on Friday night? I'm having the girls around for a little birthday celebration and I could do with you to help me out? It might be a late night again and I'd give you double wages like last time.'

Millie blinked. She had half feared that following the tiramisu incident as she called it, Alicia would decide not to employ her any longer. The cleaning job at Alicia's – three mornings a week - was ideal for her and it would have been a huge blow if she lost it.

'Of course I will,' she said now, giving Keely a thumbs up sign. 'What time do you want me there?'

'Seven o'clock. It's just a simple dinner, not so elaborate as the last time but I do want it served up nicely. Have you found a white apron to go over that black dress you wore the other night?'

Millie stuck her tongue out at Keely who was listening to one side of the conversation with interest. 'No,' she said. 'I'll see if I can buy one before Friday.'

'Please do that,' Alicia said, preparing to sign off.

'Well, well,' Keely said later when Millie filled her in on her conversation with Alicia. 'You must have made an impression on the hoi polloi.'

'I doubt it,' Millie said with a laugh. 'The money will come in handy. I just hope Mrs Donovan doesn't get shirty about being asked to babysit again so soon.'

'I wish I could help but I'm on night duty.' Keely said. She was a nurse at an old people's home not far from where she lived.

'I know. Don't worry. Mrs D. usually comes up trumps.'

'You might get one of Alicia's friends giving you some work,' Keely said. 'This could be the making of you, my girl.'

Millie rolled her eyes theatrically. 'Yeah, sure. I'll be the go-to waitress in Greenfields.'

Her phone rang again. It was Mrs Foley.

'Could you do me a favour, love? Could you look after the shop for me on Friday night? My sister is in hospital and I want to go and see her. I'll be late getting back so if you could help out, it would be great.'

Millie sometimes helped out in Mrs Foley's shop, it was something she enjoyed doing. Maeve and Danny usually tagged along. They loved playing with Daffy, the cat.

Millie bit her lip. 'Oh, I'm so sorry, Mrs Foley. I've got a job waitressing for Alicia Scott-Douglas this Friday night. I'd be free any other evening, though.'

'That's a pity. Can't be helped. No worries. I'll shut the shop for the evening.'

'I'm really sorry,' Millie said again and meant it. She was very fond of Mrs Foley, who had welcomed her to the area with open arms when she fled Kevin and ended up here. It was Mrs Foley who had spread the word among her customers that Millie was available for cleaning jobs.

'It never rains but it pours,' Millie said to Keely when she had put the phone down. 'Either nothing is happening or I'm wanted in three places at once. I'd have much preferred helping out in the shop than in snobby Alicia Scott-Douglas' kitchen. She must have been pleased with me last time and she did pay me good money for the night.'

'And you do need the money,' Keely reminded her. 'I don't suppose Mrs Foley can pay you much.'

Millie pulled a face. 'I don't take any money from her, I mean, we're neighbours. But I do want to replace the dodgy boiler, once I'm sure we won't be evicted.'

CHAPTER SEVENTEEN

'You know that concert I'm organizing for The Haven Cat and Dog rescue?' Sherry said as she dropped her handbag onto a chair in Zac's kitchen. She had popped in on him on her way home from work although it was late. He was always pleased to see her and sometimes sitting chatting to him about the things that were bothering her, no matter how trivial, was the best part of the day. 'That group PeppityPep who promised to come and do it all for free has just cancelled and it's too late to find anyone else. Could you rock up with your group and play for us?'

'Second best, that's me,' he said and although he grinned at her, she felt suddenly that there was more to his remark than appeared. 'Before I say yes, I need to know when and where.' He placed two steaming mugs of tea on the kitchen table.

Sherry took a sip of the scalding liquid and pulled a face. 'I need more milk in this if you're not to set me on fire.'

'Sorry, I've run out. You'll have to blow on it or wait until it cools a bit.'

'I'll let you have some milk if you want. I know I've got half a carton in my fridge. In exchange for a yes on the concert front. It's on this Saturday night.'

Zac laughed. 'You drive a hard bargain, lady, but yes, OK. I actually don't have any plans. I'll get the guys together and we'll rock the night away for you. That should keep you in cat food. Why are you working so late?' he added. 'You look a bit frazzled any time I see you these days.'

'What a wonderful compliment.' Sherry laughed back at him. 'I'm working on this report for my boss Piers Halloran. If he likes it, I might get to go to Paris and open an office there.'

'Paris. Ooh, la la. What does Mike think of that?'

Sherry shrugged. 'He's leaving it up to me.'

'I see.' He looked at her. 'Is it worth knocking yourself out, though? Would you really chuck everything and take off for Paris if you were offered the job?'

'I don't know,' she admitted. 'Sometimes, I wonder why I'd hang on here. Maybe I need a new challenge.'

'A bit drastic though. Or do you think that Mike might up stakes and follow you to Paris?'

'I don't know what to think. In any case my dear colleague Vicky will most likely get the preference. She's always trying her charms on Piers. It's yes sir, no sir, three bags full sir. Makes him feel like an alpha male instead of a pain-at-the-base-of-the-spine.'

They both laughed. She had told Zac about the difficulties she was experiencing working for Piers. 'I need to clone,' she had said. 'I need to be two people doing two things at the same time: the financial report from last month and the proposed budget figures for next year and if I'm really in form, do my own job as well and smile into the bargain.'

'Things will work out,' Zac said now in his quiet way. 'By Christmas, you'll know what you want to do.'

The thing was, Sherry was not sure herself what exactly she wanted to do.

CHAPTER EIGHTEEN

When she looked back on that afternoon outing with Ross, Jessica was surprised at how relaxed and confident she felt in his company despite her original qualms of being out with a man on her own after all her years of marriage. She had had some thoughts of making a last minute excuse not to go as she drove her car back to park at her cottage with Ross following. Am I crazy? She asked herself. He'd said "no strings attached" but did he really mean that? Supposing things went wrong? But no, she felt sure he did not need to force himself on anyone. He was attractive, had oodles of charm and could have any woman he wanted, she felt sure. Besides, he knew she was married.

Trouble is, she told herself as she alighted from her car, the trouble is that I have never been on a date since I met Owen. He was my first and only love. I have no idea what to expect from a casual afternoon drive.

She waved expressively at Ross to indicate that she'd be right back and dashed indoors to refresh her make-up, comb her hair and yes, to take two quick swigs of gin straight from the bottle in the kitchen. She rinsed her mouth out at the sink and then applied fresh lipstick in front of the hall mirror.

'I was afraid you'd vanish, like a princess in a fairy tale,' Ross said with a smile as she got into the passenger seat beside him. 'You're too good to be true, you know that, Jessica?'

She felt the colour rush into her cheeks – thank goodness for make-up – and although her hands were shaking, she managed to give a reasonably genuine laugh. It was better not to offer any sort of comment, she decided.

'Where are we going for this drive?' she asked instead.

'I thought we might do a little tour of the coast,' he said. 'I know a really nice seafood restaurant where we can eat later. That's if you like seafood?'

'I love seafood,' she told him. Sawdust would taste like ambrosia in his company.

'Good girl. OK, let's go.'

When Ross said a tour of the coast, he had meant just that. He chose quiet backroads and stopped occasionally so that they could take in some of the really beautiful views. She would have liked to get out and walk a bit but that did not seem to be in Ross' itinerary. She could not quite banish the feeling that he had taken a lot of women on this coastal tour. Then she chided herself for being silly. She was not a "date" like the other women would have been.

They had a delicious meal at a small out-of-the-way restaurant where the staff seemed to know him and then it was time to drive home. He said a chaste goodnight, not attempting to get close to her, and waited until she was inside her cottage before he drove off.

Jessica looked at herself in the hall mirror, her eyes were sparkling, her cheeks glowing and she could not put it all down to the wine she had drunk at dinner even if her head was starting to spin.

One thing frightened her. If Ross had suggested he come in for a nightcap, she would have said yes and she wasn't sure where it would have ended. I need to get a grip, she told herself.

CHAPTER NINETEEN

On the Friday evening, Millie prepared for her stint at Alicia Scott-Douglas's house. Yep, that white apron she'd managed to find in the thrift shop in Greenfields shopping mall looked good with the black dress. There was a small stain on the hem - red wine maybe? - but with a bit of luck, no one would notice. They'd all be too busy bitching about their other friends, she reckoned.

She stuck her tongue out at her reflection. 'Waitress of the year award goes to Millie Bennett,' she said aloud.

'What? Did you say something love?' Mrs Donovan called from the sitting room where she was ensconced on the sofa with the children lying on the rug in front of the old-fashioned fireplace. They were engrossed in colouring in pictures in the books which Millie had bought them this morning. Millie hoped that would keep them occupied until it was time for Mrs Donovan to read a story and put them to bed. It was Danny's turn to pick which story would be read tonight so there would be a disagreement at some stage, as Millie knew only too well. No doubt she would hear all about it in the morning.

'I was just talking to myself, Mrs D,' she said now, checking her watch. 'I'd better get going or I'll be late. Thanks a million again for helping out.'

She kissed the children goodnight and hurried out onto the street buttoning her coat as she went. Alicia Scott-Douglas inspected her from top to toe when she arrived and although she did not offer any comment, she give a slight nod as if satisfied with Millie's attire.

Alicia Scott-Douglas' friend Samantha was one of the ladies invited to the birthday party and she smiled a greeting at Millie. There were six women in all and Millie heard bits of their conversation as she served them.

'Your cousin Ross seems to have hit it off with that new lady from Fernwood Cottages,' one of the women said and Alicia laughed. 'Oh, Ross is a lady killer. Always out for adventure. I did warn him that she's a married woman and a local at that, so I hope he behaves.' 'She's old enough to look out for herself,' someone else observed, 'dressed for adventure the other night,' said another voice, 'she certainly scored with Ross, hope her husband doesn't mind'. Eventually the conversation drifted to others of their acquaintance. Women and gossip, Millie thought to herself with an inner smile. She had not taken to Jessica Clifford but she felt almost sorry for her for being the subject of bitchy comments.

The evening passed off reasonably well. Millie was kept very busy but at least now she knew the routine and what was expected of her. Her thoughts turned to Mrs Foley now and again. She had noticed that the shop was closed when she left home this evening. Mrs Foley had obviously not found anyone to stand in for her while she visited her sister today. It was the first time Millie had not been able to help out in the shop and although there was nothing she could do about it, she still felt a twinge of guilt. How lucky these women were, she thought, as she served up the main course and listened to their chatter. They were all well off, not dependent on the income from a small shop or a cleaning job. They all had husbands who provided for them.

That train of thought brought her inevitably to what was uppermost in her mind these days. Would Jason DeVries, their new landlord turn them all out of Fernwood Cottages and if he did, what would she do? She loved her little cottage. It had proved a safe haven when she left Kevin and above all she loved the feeling of belonging to a community. At this stage she knew everyone – or nearly everyone if you excluded Jessica Clifford. Everybody was accepted no matter how eccentric they were. Mrs Donovan, always full of everyone's business, Mad Bobby, who had been a priest at one time if you believed local gossip, and his pal Jimbo whose father and grandfather had worked on Fernwood Estate, Lady Moll a former English teacher, Zac who played the guitar and survived doing odd jobs and did all the heavy lifting for his neighbours, Sherry who had a really posh job in the city but who had time for everyone. They all called Fernwood Cottages home.

Here her train of thought was interrupted by Alicia coming to pay her for her night's work. Definitely the best part of the night, she thought as she stowed the money away in the inner pocket of her anorak. She smiled to herself as she stacked the dishwasher and prepared to do a final clear up.

It was too late to get the bus which meant that she was faced with the twenty-odd minute walk home. The wind had risen, driving the rain into her face like last week, only this time she had dressed for the bad weather. She pulled the hood of her anorak tighter and set off at a brisk pace. The children would be asleep and tomorrow being Saturday they didn't have to get up early. A nice cup of tea when she got home with a digestive biscuit or two, that would be heaven. She would have loved a slice of that special cheesecake which one of Alicia's friends had made for dessert. They had only eaten half of it and one little slice would have gone down nicely to round off tonight, but Alicia had not offered to let her have a piece and she did not want to ask. There had been loads of food left over, too, and she had heard Alicia telling one of her guests that she might have to throw some of it out. 'If I serve it up tomorrow, there'll be no end to the complaints' she had said with a laugh.

Millie having been brought up on the "waste not, want not" principle was annoyed. She would have been more than happy to serve it up tomorrow, there was enough left over to make a tasty dinner for herself and the children.

With thoughts like these to occupy her, Millie turned into the lane which led to Fernwood Cottages. It was a dark corner with overhanging trees now dripping rain. She almost tripped over a bundle at the side of the pavement. For a few seconds she thought that it was a heap of old rags that someone had thrown out onto the street, then she heard a moan of pain. A moment later and Millie was on her knees beside the bundle and in the uncertain light she recognized who this was.

'Mrs Foley! Oh my God! Are you hurt? What happened?'

CHAPTER TWENTY

'Is it you, love?' Mrs Foley's voice was barely a whisper. 'What happened? Did you have a fall?' Millie's heart was thumping against her ribs. How long had the other woman lain there in the rain?

'I fell. I thought I saw Daffy up at that tree there and I slipped and fell.' Mrs Foley's voice was stronger now. She tried to sit up and Millie put an arm around her shoulders to help steady her. 'I can't move me leg. I think it's broken or something.'

'All right. I'm here now and I'll ring an ambulance.' Millie was already fishing in her pocket with her free hand for her mobile but without success. Where had she put her phone? She always slipped it into her anorak pocket before she left the house. Her fingers closed around the money that Alicia Scott-Douglas had handed to her in the kitchen. The mobile wasn't there when she'd put the money away. Then she remembered. She had spoken to Mrs Donovan to say she would be on her way home shortly and she must have left her phone in the kitchen at Alicia Scott-Douglas' house. Where was she going to get help at this hour of the night? Should she leave Mrs Foley and rush home? Mrs Donovan had a mobile although she usually did not carry it with her. Yes, that was her best bet. And yet she did not want to leave the older woman here alone in the rain.

Even as the panicked thoughts raced through her head, the lights of a car picked them out as it slowed to negotiate the corner.

'What's going on?' the driver lowered the passenger side window and looked at them. He recognized Millie in the same moment she recognized him. Jason DeVries.

'It's Mrs Foley from the shop,' she said. 'She's had a fall and she thinks her leg is broken. We need to ring an ambulance.'

DeVries got out of the car and came round to them. 'Best thing is that I drive her to the hospital, it will be quicker for one thing,' he said. 'Give me a hand to get her in the car.'

'I'm not sure we should move her,' Millie said doubtfully. 'She might have other injuries.'

'She'll get pneumonia if she has to wait for an ambulance. Come on, give me a hand.'

He spoke gently to Mrs Foley before gathering her up in his arms and carefully placing her on the front seat of his car. Then he turned to Millie. 'Get in. You know her best. You'll be able to give the A&E people details.'

Millie hesitated, aware of Mrs Donovan expecting her back at any minute. The sight of Mrs Foley's pinched face decided her.

'All right,' she said, sliding into the rear seat. 'I'll ring the hospital and I need to ring my babysitter to let her know what's happening and I don't have my mobile on me.'

Without a word, he pulled his mobile out of his jacket pocket and handed it to her. The next moment he had started the car and was driving off. At least he seemed to know where the hospital was, she thought in relief as she thumbed in Mrs Donovan's number.

To Millie's great relief Mrs Foley was seen almost immediately. DeVries waited with Millie. She had half expected him to leave her to it once they had handed over Mrs Foley. They sat together in a small waiting room without speaking. Once Mrs Donovan learned what had happened, she volunteered to stay the night with the children if necessary. 'It's the least I can do, love,' she had said, batting away Millie's words of thanks. 'Sure isn't that what neighbours are for?'

With nothing to do but stare at the clinically cold walls of the waiting room, Millie thought the time unbearably long until a young doctor appeared.

'You're Mrs Foley's neighbours?' he asked, obviously taking them for husband and wife. 'Does she have next of kin?'

'She has a sister, but she is in hospital at the moment,' Millie told him. 'Is Mrs Foley going to be all right?'

'She has a fractured hip by the look of it and slight concussion. We will have to do some X-rays tomorrow and do a full check to see if she sustained other injuries. She told us that she slipped and fell, banging her head off a tree as she was searching for her cat.' He looked a question at them.

'I was on my way home from work when I tripped over her. That's a dark corner with all the overgrown branches and I didn't see her. Mr DeVries came along in his car just then and he decided it was better to drive straight here rather than calling an ambulance.'

The doctor consulted his notes. 'Mrs Foley will have to stay with us for the time being. She'll have to sleep in the corridor tonight but we should have a bed for her in the morning. As I said, we'll have to do a few tests tomorrow when we will know more. She asked to see you,' he continued, addressing Millie. 'The nurse will call you in a few minutes.'

Mrs Foley was lying on a trolley, looking very frail. She clutched Millie's hand. 'I can't stay here. I have to find Daffy. He's probably waiting at home for me.'

It took Millie a minute or two to register that Mrs Foley was talking about her cat.

'I'll keep an eye out for him,' she assured the other woman.

'He ran away, you see, just as I was closing up to go and see Annie, he just bolted out the front door,' Mrs. Foley went on. 'Something frightened him. I thought he'd be waiting for me when I got back and I went looking for him and then the next thing I know, I'm lying there and I can't put me left leg under me.'

Millie was mindful that the nurse had specified "a few minutes" and mentioned something about Mrs Foley getting something to settle her for the night. She knew that people who were in shock often talked non-stop when they should be relaxing. What her neighbour needed was reassurance.

'I'll look for Daffy, don't you worry,' she said. 'I'll be back later on with a nightie and toothbrush and all that kind of stuff. You get a good night's sleep and we'll talk tomorrow morning. I'll pop in to see you on the way back from dropping the kids at school.'

'Would you, love? I hope Daffy will be back and you can let him in. He's never out on his own and he likes to sleep in that chair in my sitting room.'

Millie tried to reassure her that Daffy would come home. She made a mental note to mention the cat's disappearance to Sherry, who she knew did a lot of work for The Haven Cat and Dog Rescue. If the animal was found wandering, someone might hand him in there.

A few minutes later the nurse appeared and with that way that nurses have, she soon had Mrs Foley settled with the promise that she would bring her her nightclothes and toiletries when Millie handed them in that night. Millie soon found herself being escorted back to the waiting room. To her surprise, Jason DeVries was still there.

'I'll drop you home,' he told her in that don't-argue-with-me tone he seemed to use with her.

'Thank you,' she said and wished she really meant it. I'd rather get help from Jack the Ripper, she thought to herself. Although to be fair, it was decent of him to wait and give her a lift.

'Mrs Foley is going to be all right?' He asked as they drove off.

'I hope so. They didn't seem to think she was too seriously hurt. I'll be back to the hospital later on to drop off some stuff for her and I might know more then.'

'Back to the hospital? Surely that can wait until morning?'

'Do you know how late it is? Hospitals start very early and she'll be more relaxed if she has her own nightie and toothbrush and all that.'

'All right. I'll drive you there. There won't be any buses at this time of the night or the morning, to be more exact.'

'I couldn't possibly –' she started to say but he cut her short.

'How were you planning to get there anyway? Be sensible. In fact, if you're just dropping the stuff off at the hospital, I can do it for you and you can go home to your family. You'll be visiting her later on, I gather, and by then the hospital will be able to tell you how things are with her and you'll know what she needs for a long or a short stay.'

He was right, she had to admit. She probably wouldn't get to see Mrs Foley if she went back now. 'Thank you,' she said meekly,' that sounds like a good idea.'

Why was he being so nice all of a sudden? Maybe he was hoping she wouldn't object when the cottage tenants were served their notice to quit. Nice try Mr DeVries.

As she always had the key to Mrs Foley's shop on her keyring, it was only a matter of popping upstairs and sorting a few items into a carrier bag which she then handed over to Jason.

'I'll drive you to the hospital tomorrow,' he said as she got out of his car at her own front door. 'Would ten o'clock suit you?'

This was the last thing she expected and she did not have a ready excuse for refusing his offer, so found herself spluttering her thanks. He waved a hand in dismissal and drove off.

She didn't tell him that with Mrs Donovan staying late to mind the children, she was going to search for Daffy. Mrs Foley would not be happy until she knew the little cat was safely at home again. And again, she wondered why Jason DeVries was being so kind. Did he feel some obligation to his tenants? Or was it simply a ploy to soft-soap them when his plans were revealed? Either way, she wished she did not have to see him again. He brought out the worst in her and it was hard to be polite and grateful when she really wanted to scream at him.

The rain was teeming down now. Hopefully it would dampen Daffy's lust for adventure and she'd be able to find him and bring him home.

CHAPTER TWENTY-ONE

Jessica took a few sips from the glass of gin and tonic on the dressing table before carefully applying her favourite lipstick. She took a deep breath to steady herself while her thoughts raced round in her head. What on earth had made her agree to go to a concert with Ross in aid of Haven, the cats and dogs home, of all places?

He had texted her this morning to ask if she would come with him tonight. *I have two tickets*, he had written, *Alicia tells me that one of your neighbours, Sherry, practically runs the place and we all need to chip in and help get them some money. It starts at eight so I'll collect you around seven thirty.*

Of course she could have said no, that she already had other things on but he most likely would not have believed her. She knew that the night they had dinner together, she had told him far too much about her marriage and her anger at Owen for leaving her alone in this miserable place for so long. I shouldn't have had so much wine, she told herself. I must cut down on the drinking when I'm out with Ross, otherwise I'll end up hating myself for ever.

Owen had phoned her at lunch time today as was his wont.

'I may be able to get home for Halloween,' he said. 'I'm trying my best at any rate. We could both go to Edinburgh and see the kids, do a bit of sight-seeing.'

'Halloween! That would be wonderful.' She felt her spirits lift and a rush of tenderness engulf her. It was just what she needed, a long weekend with the family.

'I can't promise now,' he warned. 'I'll do my very best. There is so much interest in my lectures that I might be invited to do a few extra presentations.'

'You mean, you're not really sure at all?' Disappointment made her words stick in her throat. 'Why bother to mention it then?'

'Look, as I said I'll do my best. I miss you and the children, you know that.' He sounded touchy as he often did during their phone calls lately. 'What have you been doing with yourself, anyway? Have you got to know your neighbours yet?'

'I haven't been doing very much.' She knew he was concerned about her, was aware that she was lonely and not happy in Fernwood Cottages. But what did that amount to? He loved his work, as she knew very well. A few months ago, before he went away, they were at a dinner together and one of his colleagues had let slip that Owen didn't actually have to make these trips, that he could delegate if he so wished. His colleague had looked embarrassed when he realized what he had said and noticed Jessica's expression and had tried to backtrack.

'Owen is so conscientious and hardworking,' he had said hastily. 'We all admire him no end.'

'Don't you believe it,' Owen had laughed when she mentioned this conversation to him. 'they'd get the whip out if I didn't go. There's no one else and let's face it, I want the project we're working on to succeed.'

And then he had changed the subject, but Jessica had not forgotten. Was Owen glad of an excuse to get away from her? He had always worked long hours but they did have the weekends together with the children. Was life with her too boring now that the children were no longer at home?

She heard voices in the background, one of them a woman's which she was sure she had heard before. 'I've got to go,' Owen said. 'I have to meet a few possible financial backers for dinner tonight and I need to go through some figures. Wish me luck.'

And with the usual "love you" to each other, he had rung off, leaving Jessica angry and hurt and lonely again.

Thinking over that conversation now, she was suddenly glad that she was going out tonight. Ross was good company. He made her laugh. He listened to her and gave her the impression that what she said was important. What was Owen doing tonight? Dinner with prospective financial backers? Or with that woman whose voice she had heard in the background? She had never in all their years of marriage had reason to suspect him of being unfaithful but now she was not sure of anything about their relationship. Or was this because of Ross? Did it stem from her own guilty conscience?

Later as she was waiting for Ross to collect her, she went to the cupboard in the kitchen and took out the bottle of gin which she stored there. There was only a quarter left. She really must stock up again even if she intended cutting down on her alcohol consumption. She stood with the bottle in her hand, willing herself to put it back in the cupboard. Well, maybe one little glass wouldn't do any harm.

CHAPTER TWENTY-TWO

'How are you, Mrs Foley?' Millie took the other woman's hand and held it lightly between both of hers. 'Did you manage to sleep last night?'

Mrs Foley's face looked as white as the pillow where her head rested. She managed a wan smile. 'I'm all right love. They're being really nice to me.'

'The doctor said you'll have to stay in hospital for a bit. You fractured your hip, he said. They want to keep you in for observation, too, seeing as how you had mild concussion.'

'They told me that.' Mrs Foley's eyes filled with tears. 'Did you find Daffy?'

'Not yet. He's around somewhere. I'll bet he'll come home when he gets hungry enough.' Millie hoped she sounded reassuring.

The truth was that she had spent hours looking for the cat with no success. She had put some food in Mrs Foley's back garden this morning in the hopes that he would stay near the shop if he came to eat.

Jason DeVries had collected her at ten o'clock to drive her to the hospital. He had assured her that he had handed over the carrier bag with Mrs Foley's night things last night and upon enquiry had been told that she was "comfortable". Although Millie found it hard to accept his help, it did save her a lot of time. Mrs Donovan had taken charge of the children in exchange for extracting from Millie as many details on Mrs Foley's accident as she could. By now, everyone in Fernwood Cottages probably knew what had happened and why the shop was shut this morning.

'I've brought you some more things, oh and your mobile phone,' Millie went on, wanting to divert the other woman's attention from her worries about the cat. 'I'll pop in at visiting time tomorrow. That will be in the afternoon, as it's Sunday.'

Mrs Foley did not seem to be listening. She plucked at the bed covers. 'Can you do me a favour, love? Can you take over the shop until I'm back on me feet? You know where everything is. The Sunday papers will be delivered early tomorrow morning. Could you open up the shop?'

Millie stared at her in dismay. Run Mrs Foley's little shop? How could she manage that with the cleaning jobs she had to do, besides getting the children to school?'

'I know it's a lot to ask,' Mrs Foley said quickly, seeing her expression. 'Listen love, you know your way around the shop. I keep money upstairs in my bedroom in the safe. I'll give you the combination. There's enough in there to pay expenses and if you want my signature on anything, sure I'm here in the hospital.'

'Well, I'm not sure. Isn't there anyone else you could ask?'

Mrs Foley shook her head. 'No one, love.' Her lips trembled and a tear gathered at the corner of her eye. 'If I have to close the shop, I'll be ruined. I'll lose all my customers. The delivery companies won't want to do business with me, they'll think I'm too much of a risk. Don't you see? I have to keep going for another couple of years.'

'Oh Mrs Foley, I'm not sure I can manage it with my other jobs. Surely someone will step in to help?'

'I know you need them jobs. I'll pay you a wage. You can take it out of the money in the safe. Please, love. I'll talk to the women you clean for and explain to them. They'll understand. I've no one else to help, love.'

The tears had spilled over now, trickling down her cheeks. She looked pale and fragile, lying there in the sterile hospital setting.

Millie felt a lump forming in her throat. She knew only too well what it was like to be on your own, to have to depend on yourself. But she was young, she had plans for her future, whereas Mrs Foley was old – in her mid-sixties, Millie guessed – and probably needed all the money she could save between now and retirement.

'All right,' she found herself saying. 'I'll do it. Don't worry, we'll get it all sorted out.'

Jason DeVries was waiting for her in the Reception area of the hospital.

'Everything all right?' he wanted to know as he escorted her to where he had parked his car.

Millie shrugged. 'I spoke to the doctor. Mrs Foley will have to stay in hospital for a week at least. The fracture is complicated, he said. And she suffered a mild concussion. Since she doesn't have anyone at home to look after her, they want to keep her in. The doctor said she will need to go into a nursing home for a bit when she's discharged. I didn't mention that to her because she's so upset already.'

He opened the passenger door for her and then slid into the driving seat. He did not start the engine straight away, instead he turned to look at her. 'You do take things to heart, don't you? It's not necessarily your problem, is it?'

How could anyone be so callous? 'She's my neighbour,' she said, close to tears, 'she has no family apart from her sister who's in hospital. There's no one else to help her.'

'Surely there are social services?'

'Right now, she needs people around her that she knows. Everything else can be sorted later.'

He started the car and eased it carefully out of the hospital car park. 'Obviously it's upsetting but what can you do? You've already been very kind in getting her overnight things sorted. I daresay the hospital will get her the necessary help.'

Millie made no answer and they drove back in silence. He stopped outside her cottage and turned to her as if to say something but with a 'thanks for the lift', she stormed out of the car. What a selfish, callous person, she thought. She watched him drive off and then she hurried to Mrs Foley's shop in the hopes that Daffy would be waiting there. There was no sign of him, however. How could she ever break it to Mrs Foley if something had happened to him?

CHAPTER TWENTY-THREE

Sherry wondered sometimes if she was experiencing what she had heard referred to as "burn out syndrome". She had stayed up very late last night working on the various reports Piers wanted from her. Today she was so tired that her body ached. She had started work on the presentation for setting up an office in Paris but in the end was so tired she had to leave it. She was determined that it should be the very best, far better than whatever Vicky would produce. No half measures. Even if she wasn't sure she'd take the job in Paris if she was offered it. If she were honest, she could not imagine living anywhere else than here in Fernwood Cottages even if a change of job would be a welcome challenge. Of course, if the new owner of Fernwood Cottages evicted them, she would have no choice but to leave. Somehow, she refused to consider this possibility, at least for the present.

The concert tonight in aid of The Haven Cats and Dogs Sanctuary had taken up a lot of her time in addition to everything else that was happening. Designing and printing posters, organizing a raffle, getting local media involved, the calls on her time and input seemed endless and sometimes she thought she would fall over. But here she was, still in one piece, still able to think and organize.

Mike had promised to come to the concert even though he had a rugby match that afternoon. They had not seen each other for over a week owing to her workload. But tonight he would be there and he would stay over, they'd have a leisurely breakfast and maybe get a takeaway and watch a film in the evening. The perfect way of winding down after this crazy week. It was too long since they had had a cozy night in together.

Sherry gave her neighbour Millie with her two children a lift to the concert which was being held in Greenfields community centre. Maeve and Danny were both excited to be allowed out so late and were full of chatter.

'Danny's going to sing for everyone,' Maeve announced.

Millie laughed. 'I'm sure everyone would be charmed but better wait to be asked,' she said.

Sherry felt a stab of envy. Even though Millie was a single mother who struggled to make ends meet, she thought how good it would be to have children, a family to care for. She pushed the negative feelings away and concentrated on getting an update on Mrs Foley.

'I more or less promised to run the shop for her,' Millie confessed. 'I haven't the faintest idea how I'm going to manage it, but I couldn't let her down.'

'What will happen to your cleaning jobs?' Sherry wanted to know.

Millie shrugged her shoulders. 'I rang round everybody today to let them know that I wouldn't be in for the time being at least. I'll have to see how it goes, I suppose.'

Sherry was silent for a few minutes, her mind running over possibilities. 'You know what? I'll make an announcement tonight at the concert saying we're looking for people to help out. Would you be okay with that?'

Millie looked at her doubtfully. 'If you think it would work.'

Sherry reached out and squeezed her arm. 'We can but try.'

CHAPTER TWENTY-FOUR

As Jessica and Ross seated themselves in the hall at the Greenfields community centre, Jessica noticed the glances cast in their direction. She thought she heard whisperings from Alicia Scott-Douglas' little group of friends who were seated across the aisle. Her cheeks were in a glow which was not only attributable to the two gins she had hastily downed before Ross collected her.

'I see my cousin Alicia and her better half have arrived,' Ross said as he lifted a hand to wave at them. 'You know that cliché about anybody who's anybody putting in an appearance?'

Jessica could think of a lot of cliches that would fit Greenfields and Fernwood Cottages in particular. 'It's good that everyone is supporting the rescue home,' was all she said, however. She twisted in her seat to give Alicia and her husband a big smile, wondering at the same time what Alicia thought of herself and Ross being here together. Did she think they were dating? And if so, what did she make of that? Samantha was part of the little group, of course, but to her relief, was too engrossed in conversation to notice her. They had not seen each other since the party at Alicia Scott-

Douglas' place for which Jessica was very grateful, not wanting to be quizzed about Ross, although eager to glean any information on him that came her way. She was most likely the subject of speculation, she reckoned and anything she said would be relayed to Alicia and their friends.

'You look really beautiful tonight,' Ross murmured, breaking in on her thoughts. 'The most attractive woman in the room.'

'Flattery will get you anywhere.' She had meant it to sound flippant but when the words were out, she thought it sounded more like a proposition and her colour deepened even more. God! That was the gin talking again. She really must cut down on her drinking.

Ross was looking at her now, his eyes twinkling. She guessed he was trying to decipher her remark. 'I mean it,' he said. 'Beautiful and intelligent. I am so glad that I was persuaded to come to that dinner party. Against my better judgement, if you want the truth. I expected it to be a dull parochial affair and then there you were.'

Jessica looked away from his gaze. She was getting into deep waters here. Time to give some kind of signal to indicate that she did not want their friendship (was that the right word?) to progress any further. She sought for a suitable remark but came up empty. A movement in front of the stage caught her attention. Sherry, her neighbour at Fernwood Cottages, appeared and placed a box of leaflets on the floor. Her words were lost in the buzz of conversation and the microphone she held in her hand did not seem to be working.

'It looks like they're selling concert programmes,' Jessica said, glad of a diversion. 'I suppose we should buy one to see what they're planning for the evening.'

Ross got up obediently and went up to the stage to buy the programmes. He handed her one as he sat down again next to her. 'Sounds like fun. All local talent. I expect you know all these people.'

'I have to admit that I don't.' She ventured a smile at him. After all, she did not want to annoy him. What was the best way to keep their relationship friendly but distanced?

'No hidden talents to charm the locals? I find that hard to believe.' He did not seem put out by her behaviour, devoting himself to reading off the list of performers.

The lights were dimmed at last and the show began with a song from a bosomy young woman who Jessica had never seen before. Ross reached across and touched her hands where they lay in her lap. 'Hallelujah. One of my favourite songs,' he whispered. 'Do you like Leonard Cohen?'

Her whole body tingled at his touch. He was looking at her now and she did not want to return his gaze. Oh god, how did she stop this from going any further?

'I like some of Leonard Cohen's work,' she said, trying hard to keep her voice neutral. 'Hallelujah is a favourite of mine, too.'

He squeezed her hands lightly and then withdrew his hand. 'I knew we were kindred spirits.'

Someone behind them said "sshhh" and they smiled at each other and turned their attention to what was happening on the stage.

In the interval, Sherry thanked them all for coming and gave a brief description of the work that the Haven Cats and Dogs Rescue did.

'Something else I'd like to mention,' she went on. 'As most of you will probably know, Mrs Foley from the shop is in hospital at the moment and we need volunteers to keep the place open. Right now, Millie is going to take over, but she can't do it all on her own. Please come and see us after the concert if you could help.'

There was a break for tea and cakes which were laid out at the back of the hall. Ross looked a question at Jessica. She shook her head. The effects of the two shots of gin were wearing off. Tea would sober her up even more.

Ross looked around at the crowd. 'Millie is the pretty girl over there, I take it? I think she was serving dinner at Alicia's place the night we met.'

Jessica was stung by the "pretty girl" epithet. Millie was pretty in her own way, she acknowledged, but not glamorous or sophisticated. Right now, she was in the act of shepherding her two children in the direction of the table with the tea and cakes. Not Ross' type, she would have thought.

'Hey, you two.' Samantha came towards them balancing a plate in one hand and a mug of tea in the other. 'Enjoying yourselves?' Her eyes darted from one to the other of them. 'I didn't know you were coming here,' she added, addressing Ross. 'I thought you told me you hated local talent concerts.'

'Well, I changed my mind.' He grinned at her.

Samantha made a face at him. 'Don't forget that Jessica here is a happily married woman.'

For some reason, Jessica resented that remark.

Later, Ross seemed in the best of spirits as they drove home after the concert. 'Some of that stuff was really good,' he said, 'that band The Wallows was super. Who'd have thought there was so much talent around?'

He pulled up outside the cottage and looked across at her. 'I really enjoyed tonight,' he said softly. 'Seems a shame to end it here and now.'

Jessica's heart started to race like a mad thing. She wanted him to take her in his arms and kiss her senseless and -.
Hastily she pulled herself up. No, she told herself. No and no and no. She pulled open the car door and got out. 'Thank you, Ross, I really enjoyed tonight.'

'Not even a goodnight kiss?' He asked in that soft, sexy voice.

'Goodnight,' she said and hurried up the path to the safety of her front door.

If I'd had a few more gins, she thought as she stepped into the little kitchen, who knows what would have happened? I'm just a few gins away from making a huge mistake.

CHAPTER TWENTY-FIVE

Mike did not show up for the concert. During the evening, Sherry checked her mobile once or twice but there was no message from him. Had something happened to him? He had promised he'd come. She had been looking forward to their time together after the concert tonight.

At the interval she sent him a WhatsApp message. *See you later on. Xxx.*

For the next hour or more, she was kept busy backstage making sure all the various performers were on cue. Kitty, their star soprano had a row with the pianist before the concert started and it was all Sherry could do to smooth things over. Mad Bobby, having had a few drinks, was insisting on giving his rendition of "Oh Danny Boy" and she was forced to let him do that, despite her better judgement. He accepted the applause and wolf whistles from the audience with a gracious if wobbly bow and it was all she could do to stop him singing a second song.

Zac, dependable as always, arrived early with his group the Wallows and they filled in any gaps between the various acts with a medley of rock and roll and more currently popular songs. They got the longest applause of the evening, which annoyed Kitty who considered herself a very superior artist. Rob, the piano player, made some snide remark about people thinking they were performing in *La Scala* in Milan and it took another huge effort from Sherry to calm things down.

At the end of the night, a number of people came to offer their services in running Mrs Foley's shop. The Donovans, Mad Bobby, even the elusive Jimbo, who was rarely seen in public, all came forward to speak to herself and Millie. They would work out a rota, they decided and agreed to meet in the shop next day.

'We'll take it from there,' Sherry said. 'thank you so much to you all. See you tomorrow at eleven o'clock in the shop.'

When everyone had gone and volunteers from The Haven had started to tidy up, Sherry sat down at the back of the hall and pulled out her mobile to see if Mike had answered her message.

Sorry, can't make it after all, talk soon, he had written.

She sat and stared at the words. No explanation. No apology for not being there to support her. He knew that tonight was important to her – she had told him often enough during their brief phone conversations this past week. He knew how important The Haven's work was and how much effort she had put in to get this concert off the ground. Surely he could have made time? Surely tonight should have been a priority? If Mike was involved in something like that, she would have made sure she was there to support him, she knew.

She had been looking forward to a romantic weekend with Mike. And now she was faced with going back to her empty cottage and she did not even know if he would show up tomorrow.

'What's the matter?'

Zac's voice startled her. She had not heard him approach. 'Nothing.' She sat up straighter and forced a smile at him. 'Just taking time out.'

He sat down beside her. 'Obviously there's something. My guess is it has to do with Mike. Am I right?'

She sometimes thought that Zac could read her mind. She swallowed hard to get rid of the lump that suddenly formed in her throat. Any minute now and the floodgates would open and all her insecurities about Mike and their relationship would come pouring out. The community hall at Greenfields was certainly not the place for these kinds of dramatics. Besides that, she fought against showing any sign of weakness to anyone, not even to her three best friends. She had been brought up on the "chin up" philosophy. She found it hard to meet Zac's steady gaze.

'Relax,' he said. 'Give yourself a bit of rope. You've been going like the clappers all week. Every time I see you, you're dashing home from work to do more work and you've been up to your neck in getting this concert off the ground. You're only human, Sherry.'

She swallowed hard, fighting for control and only when she felt that her emotions were on an even keel did she speak. 'It is about Mike,' she said quietly, 'I was sure he'd come. He didn't even try and make an excuse.' She stood up before he could reply. 'Sorry, Zac, sorry for burdening you with my problems.'

'Tell you what, Sher, you get cleaned up, we'll finish up here and then go and have a drink at my place. Get it out of your system to talk about it.'

He was right, she knew. Although she had never gone into detail about her relationship, she always felt that Zac understood that despite all her efforts to appear content with the situation, she loved Mike and wanted a commitment from him. Maybe it would be good to finally admit her insecurities, bring it all out in the open.

However, by the time she had helped the Haven volunteers to complete tidying up the hall, she had changed her mind. She was just overworked, she told herself. What she needed was a good night's sleep. Mike would no doubt show up tomorrow with a satisfactory explanation for his absence tonight – he had made no secret of the fact that he was not into concerts like the one she was organizing. 'Oldie music and a bit of opera' was how he put it. 'Stuff for widows and pensioners.'

'Let's leave tonight, Zac,' she said as she prepared to lock up. 'I'd only be a dead weight. You played a blinder tonight and it wouldn't be fair of me to dump my love life problems on you.'

'Oh, well, you know best.' She thought he looked – what? Disappointed? 'I'll see you around.' And he took off in rapid strides.

She watched him go with troubled eyes. She did not want to hurt his feelings. He was the best friend she had ever had. Always there for her, ready to build her up when she was down. She confided almost all her troubles to Zac. Almost all. Her relationship with Mike was not up for heart-to-hearts with anyone. Sherry felt a stab of compunction. Zac was only trying to help, after all. Unlike Mike, he was always there when she needed him.

CHAPTER TWENTY-SIX

Sherry dropped Millie and her children off at the shop on the way home. Millie wanted to check if Daffy had returned, but there was no sign of him. She was going to have to find him somehow or other, she decided as she walked to her cottage. Mrs Foley would be heartbroken without him.

Later, she tucked her two children into bed and saw them drift off to sleep, tired from their night out at the concert. Then, armed with a torch and some cat treats, she stole out of the cottage and started her search for the animal. The food she had left out was gone, she noted, but that did not mean that he had eaten it, there were other cats and indeed other animals, including rats, who might very well have helped themselves to the food.

She searched the area around the shop and the cottages, softly calling "Daffy". It was dark and cold. More than likely he had eaten the food she left out this evening and had found a cosy spot to curl up in for the night. She stood still, listening to the night sounds: leaves rustling in the light breeze, a car revving its engine in the distance. There was just one more place she could try and that was the outhouses at Fernwood House, which was now out of bounds according to the new owner. It was unlikely that he lived there, Millie decided. The entrance gates had not been repaired, they still sagged open on rusty hinges. It was worth a try. She walked slowly up the driveway.

'Daffy, treats,' she cooed into the darkness. 'Come on lad, time you came back home.'

She was in view of the house now with its boarded-up windows and general air of neglect. There was no sign of Jason Devries' BMW, to her relief. He had not been at the concert or if he had, she had not seen him. The stables and other outhouses were round the back. More than likely that was where the cat was. She stopped to listen again, calling softly to Daffy and shaking the bag of treats. She thought she heard a miaow in the general direction of what used to be the dairy, a small building set apart from the others where in the good old days, butter had been churned and used in the household. She headed in that direction.

To her relief, the door to the dairy was not locked. She pushed it open, the banshee-like screech of rusty hinges making her jump. As she did so, a little body came charging towards her and scampered into the blackness. At almost the same moment, the headlights of a car flooded the yard, blinding her as she turned in dismay. The cat had already disappeared into the group of trees which bordered the yard.

The slam of the car door sounded very loud in the stillness. There was the crunch of footsteps and then a voice which was all too familiar by now.

'What in the name of all that's holy are you doing here at this time of night?'

He loomed over her in the darkness so that she could not see his expression. Not that she wanted to look at him, his tone of voice was enough.

Finally, she found her voice. 'I- I'm looking for Daffy, Mrs Foley's cat.'

'You're *what*?'

'I know I shouldn't be here, but she is so worried about him. She was looking for him when she had that fall. He's an indoor cat. He won't be able to look after himself.'

'Why do you think the cat is here?'

'I don't know.' She was close to tears now. She swallowed hard. 'I've looked everywhere and there's no sign of him. I have to find him.'

She heard the sigh he gave – he probably meant that she should. 'It's the middle of the night, for god's sake.'

She put a hand up to brush away the tear that trickled down her face. 'All right. I'm going. I know I'm trespassing.'

'Aren't you overdoing it? The cat will find his own way home. Why get so involved in things you can't solve?'

'Because I live here.'

'What does that mean, exactly?'

'We all need a place to belong. I belong here as does Mrs Foley and her cat if it comes to that.'

He stood there, saying nothing. No doubt he did not understand what she meant. She cast a look in his direction as she stepped past him. 'If you do see a cat, he's black with a teeny bit of white on one paw, could you let me know? I'd be very grateful. I could come and catch him. That is if you don't mind me doing that.'

The words came out in a rush, she was fighting to keep her voice steady and another tear was inching its way down her face. 'Good night,' she added, feeling foolish and angry with him at the same time. He wasn't the kind of person who could understand how an old woman like Mrs Foley would feel about her pet, that much was obvious.

'Good night,' he said.

She thought he was about to say something else but she did not give him a chance, hurrying away as if the hounds of hell – or of Fernwood House – were nipping at her heels.

CHAPTER TWENTY-SEVEN

'Nice of you to show up.' Sherry knew her voice was shrill but was powerless to change her tone.

Mike had appeared this morning just as she was having a lonely breakfast. He had tried to give her a "good morning" kiss, but she had batted him away. She was too angry to welcome any attempt at making up. This was not the first time he had let her down. A sleepless night had given her the opportunity to review their five and more years together and she had re-lived them all last night.

He stood looking at her, no doubt trying to gauge the best way to react. 'Look, I'm really sorry. It got so late and to be honest I'd had a few drinks so there was no way I was going to drive over.'

'Well, thanks so much for your support.' She glared at him.

'I'm here now. I can't say more than sorry.' When she made no answer, he went on. 'Tell me, how did the concert go? Did you make a lot of money for The Haven?'

'Why do you want to know? If you were genuinely interested, you'd have come with me and helped out.'

He gave a gusty sigh. 'All right. I'm a selfish bastard. Let me make it up to you tonight.'

'You wish.'

'What do you want me to do? Go on my hands and knees? What's the matter with you anyway? I'm sure you had a good time last night. You know all these people. I expect you'll be in the local paper or maybe on the local news. And you deserve it. You've worked really hard.'

He would try to kiss her again in a few minutes, she knew. Only this time, the charm wasn't working. Maybe she was just tired, too much on at work and too much effort put into making the concert a success. Whatever the reason, she did not feel like making up. Not now anyway.

She caught sight of the old-fashioned clock above the cooker. It was quarter to eleven. She had a meeting with the neighbours at eleven to discuss how to keep Mrs Foley's shop open. She stood up from the table, put her cup and plate away in the kitchen sink.

'I have to go,' she said. 'Everyone is meeting down at the shop in the minute.'

'OK, another project, is that it? Well, suit yourself but don't expect me to hang around until you find the time for me.'

Before she could reply, he had turned and stalked out the front door, banging it shut behind him. She went to the window to watch him drive off. She felt a vague sense of guilt. Was she doing too much and not leaving enough room in her life for their relationship? But no, he was the one who had not showed up last night. As so often in the past, he had managed to make her feel that it was all her fault. She just had to convince herself that this was not true.

CHAPTER TWENTY-EIGHT

Jessica had just emerged from the shower when there was a knock at the front door. Who on earth was calling so early? Not Ross, surely? Last night he had mentioned something about taking her out for lunch but they had not agreed a time. She hesitated, loathe for him to see her without make-up and probably looking a fright. There was another knock, louder this time. Perhaps it was something urgent although she could not image what that could be. She twisted the towel around her wet hair, tightened the belt on her dressing gown and went to answer.

Her nosy neighbour Mrs Donovan was standing on the doorstep, looking crisp and wide awake in her best Sunday coat. 'Are you coming to the meeting at the shop?' she said without preamble.

Jessica blinked. 'Meeting? At the shop?'

'Yeh.' Mrs Donovan looked her up and down from towel wrapped head to bare feet. 'Sure an' you were at the concert last night when Sherry asked us all to come this morning.'

'Oh,' Jessica reached up and twisted the towel around her head more tightly. She vaguely recalled something being said about meeting up at Mrs Foley's shop but to be honest, she had not paid much attention. What her neighbours did was nothing to do with her. 'I'd forgotten. Anyway, I didn't say I was coming to the meeting.'

Mrs Donovan snorted. 'All we want is to help out while Mrs Foley is in hospital. Millie can't do it all on her own.'

The woman was really the limit. I should close the door in her face, Jessica thought. 'What am I supposed to help out with as you put it?'

'Well, we'll find that out when we go to the meeting, won't we?'

Cheeky cow. 'Look, I have other things to do with my time. I'm sure you'll all come up with the perfect solution. And now, if you'll excuse me.'

Mrs Donovan did not move, simply stared impassively at her. 'You're not coming to the meeting, is that what you're saying?'

The woman was quick, that was for sure, Jessica thought angrily. What bit of "no" hadn't she understood?

'No, I'm not coming,' she said and this time she closed the door firmly. She heard the other woman shuffle away, muttering to herself.

Now why do I feel guilty? She asked herself later as she got dressed and applied make-up. I don't want anything to do with these people. Yes, it would be a shame if that shop had to close, it was very handy if you forgot to buy milk or butter or washing powder, as had been the case last week. But the supermarket at Greenfields was open and it was no trouble to drive down there if you really needed something. In any case, she thought, what can I do really? I doubt if I'd be much good working in a little shop like Mrs Foley's. I've never worked in my life.

Her mobile beeped and she walked through to the kitchen to answer it. It was Owen. He sounded very wide awake and very upbeat.

'Hallo sweetheart. How are you? Did you enjoy the concert last night?'

'Yes, it was fun. Lots of local talent. What about you? How was that business dinner?'

'Very satisfactory.'

He went on to tell her in detail, talking about future projects, funding, opportunities until she began to lose interest. When Owen got on his hobby horse, there was no stopping him and she had given up listening some time ago. She was busy wondering if Ross would simply come round or phone her first. Hopefully he wasn't too miffed at her not inviting him in last night.

'That's enough shop for one day,' Owen said as if divining that her attention had strayed. 'What are you doing today, Jess? You should get out in the fresh air. What's the weather like?'

She glanced through the kitchen window at the grey clouds scudding before a cold October wind. 'Not very inviting for a walk,' she said with a laugh. 'There's a meeting about Mrs Foley's shop. I told you that she had an accident, didn't I?'

'Oh, you're going to the meeting? Good idea. Tell Mrs Foley I was asking about her and wish her a speedy recovery from me. The cottage people are the salt of the earth.'

Jessica could have thought of other ways to describe them but all she said was, 'I might go. I'm not sure that I can contribute much, mind you.'

'Of course you can. You're a clever woman, that's why I fell for you.' She could tell he was smiling. 'And anyway, it's good to take an interest in these things.'

'I'll see.'

'You know what, you've been so good about my being away so long and everything, that I think we should take a week or ten days off in Tenerife or the South of France when I come home. A second honeymoon. What do you say?'

'That would be terrific. But when *are* you coming home?'

'I won't be able to make Halloween but right now, it looks like the first week of November or the second week at the latest. I miss you, Jess.'

Somehow, she had not believed he would be home for Halloween so her disappointment was short-lived. 'The first week of November? Why that's not far away.'

'It's not definite yet, and I might have to come back here afterwards. But I'm really doing my best to make it happen. Why don't you start looking up somewhere romantic, hot sun, hot sand, hot nights? What do you say?'

She felt a glow all over her body. Owen was the love of her life, why did she ever even doubt that? 'I'll start straight away.'

'Good. No expense spared. Can't wait. I love you, Jess.'

'I love you, too.' And she meant it.

CHAPTER TWENTY-NINE

Although Millie was not keen to be in the spotlight, she found herself practically chairing the meeting in Mrs Foley's shop. Having helped out on numerous occasions, she knew how the place was run and what would be needed to keep it functioning properly. She had arrived early so that she could take delivery of the Sunday newspapers. The shop was very popular with customers who lived some distance away showing up to buy their favourite newspaper rather than driving the two odd kilometres to the Greenfields Shopping Centre.

She had some difficulty in creating space for the participants. Sherry and Zac both arrived together to help her set up as many chairs as they could find in the place. Mrs Foley lived upstairs but as she favoured shabby sofas to simpler forms of furniture, there was not much choice of seating. Zac had brought a few spare chairs from his cottage and lined them up with the others which helped somewhat.

Millie left the twins upstairs in the little living room, lying on the carpet and colouring pictures in the books she had brought with her. They were quite happy, at least for the time being, and nodded obediently when she explained that they must not touch anything in the room.

People were starting to arrive, including one or two customers who did not know that the shop was closed for the next few hours. Millie served them, explained that all would be back to normal soon, and then finally perched herself on the counter near the till, aware of all eyes turned on her. She was pleased to see that the people from Fernwood Cottages had come, with the exception of their new neighbour Jessica Clifford. The Donovans were there, of course, with Mad Bobby seated behind them, Jimbo who mostly kept to himself had shown up, Lady Moll or Mrs Granger to give her her proper name was there as well, having just returned from Mass in Greenfields little church. She was a retired schoolteacher and very disapproving of Mad Bobby and his drinking habits and of Jimbo and his rough language. Millie knew them all and their shortcomings. She did the shopping for Mad Bobby and Jimbo and listened to Lady Moll's diatribes on The State of the Country. She would be forever grateful to Lady Moll for giving her her love of poetry – 'the best way to think' as she so often put it when quoting the old poets. There were a few other vaguely familiar faces to which Millie could not put a name. These were people who lived further away but used the shop frequently.

Before the meeting kicked off there was a good deal of talk about the future, especially among the tenants of Fernwood Cottages. Would they really be turfed out of their homes by their new landlord? To date no one had heard anything specific, in fact Millie was the only one of them to have had any contact with Jason DeVries and she had nothing to report, having never had the courage to ask him what his plans for the cottages were.

Sherry signalled that the meeting should begin and handed over to Millie.

'Thank you all for coming,' Millie said, 'as you know Mrs Foley will be in hospital for a bit and then she'll have to recuperate. She wants to keep the shop open. That means we'll all have to help out even if it's only for a few hours.'

She went on to list the times and the things that needed to be done. Sherry who was leaning on the counter beside her made notes on a pad.

'I'll come down in the evenings,' Jimbo volunteered, much to everyone's surprise. He had a drink problem, as his neighbours kindly put it, and normally kept himself very much to himself.

'Thanks, Jimbo.' Millie smiled at him but at the back of her mind, she knew that he was completely unreliable.

She looked around at the others. 'We'll need help taking deliveries and stacking the shelves,' she said.

'I'd love to help,' Podge Donovan said, 'but me back is giving me so much trouble that I can't lift anything.' He looked around the room in search of sympathy which was not forthcoming. Everyone knew that Podge was a dodger, that his wife did all the work and ran the household.

'I can take care of your kids in the afternoons if you want to work in the shop,' Mrs Donovan put in now quickly, as always covering up for her husband's shortcomings. 'If you like I can bring them to school, too. Mind you,' she added, 'the Halloween break is coming up soon so I suppose you won't need me until school starts again.'

'I'll take the deliveries and stack the stuff,' Zac said quietly. 'I'm usually around, so if you need anything, just give me a shout.'

At least she could rely on him, Millie thought in relief.

'I can do the evening shift a few times.' Sherry volunteered. She was busy scribbling in her notepad.

Mad Bobby said nothing, simply took it all in. Mrs Donovan claimed that he walked around the neighbourhood all night. 'He's as mad as a pike,' she often said. He was an odd character but always the perfect gentleman. The story that he had formerly been a priest, had most likely had a grain of truth in it, Millie often thought.

When the meeting was over, Millie, Sherry and Zac went through the names of the volunteers and the time schedules assigned to them.

'There's just one thing worrying me,' Millie said. 'I had a quick look in the till and in the safe upstairs where Mrs Foley keeps the money for the shop. There isn't much there. I found her latest bank statement and that doesn't look too good either. I think she's been making a loss for some time now.'

She did not add that she needed a reasonable income to replace that from her cleaning jobs, something that had been overlooked by the others, she felt. She would try to fit in some hours, especially for Alicia Scott-Douglas, being the most lucrative.

'Somehow that doesn't surprise me,' Sherry said. 'You know, a lot could be done to the shop to attract more customers. A coffee machine, hot food, that kind of thing. People often stop here on their way towards the motorway or if they're taking a drive down the coast road.'

'At any rate, we'll just about manage to keep the place going,' Millie said slowly. 'I'll talk to Mrs Foley when I visit her today. She'll be pleased that we're going to manage the shop for her. Now if only her cat would turn up, everything would be fine.'

CHAPTER THIRTY

Next morning, the dreaded letters arrived from Jason DeVries' estate agent, informing the tenants that they were being given six months' notice to quit and kindly referring them to a paragraph in their rental contracts which stated that they had signed their agreement to this clause when they had rented their cottages.

Mrs Donovan looked in on Millie in the shop on her way back from bringing Maeve and Danny to school. She had met the postman and taken delivery of Millie's and her own letters. They both looked over the correspondence together, the shop being empty of customers.

'Glory be to all the saints,' Mrs Donovan said when they had finished reading and stood staring at each other, dismay written all over their faces. 'How are we supposed to find any place to live? Six months' notice – what does it say – to give us enough time to find other accommodation. What a cheek. '

Millie nodded in agreement. 'Somehow I was hoping that we wouldn't hear anything, that maybe Mrs Foley had got the wrong end of the stick from those workmen who told her.'

Mrs Donovan sniffed. 'Well now we know.'

They were interrupted by the postman who came to deliver the mail to the shop. There were a few bills which Millie put to one side, seizing on the by now familiar envelope with the estate agent's name printed on it. Mrs Foley had given her permission to open everything that came. She ripped it open in the slight hope that the shop would be spared. It was a business, after all, and necessary to the neighbourhood. When she glanced through it, she saw however that the wording was identical to what she herself had received.

'Mrs Foley is going to be heartbroken,' she said.

Mrs Donovan sniffed again. 'You went to see her last evening with Zac, I think? He's a great lad, isn't he?'

'Yes, Zac drove me to the hospital but he didn't come in, just waited until I was finished my visit. We thought it would be too much for her at the minute. He'll take me there any time I want he says.'

'Like I said, a great lad, a blessing to us all.'

She could picture Mrs Donovan telling the neighbours about her getting a lift from Zac and a possible romance between them. Which was never going to happen. She was fond of him but there was no spark between them. Mrs Donovan would never believe it.

'They're going to operate on Mrs Foley's hip on Friday. It's a complicated fracture and she'll be on crutches for quite a while, so the doctor said.' Millie's voice trailed off. She was thinking of the cleaning jobs she had had to cancel and of the extra work involved in running the shop. And now this extra blow, the biggest problem of all. If Jason DeVries had come in the shop door at that moment, she would have breathed fire all over him.

CHAPTER THIRTY-ONE

Sherry read the letter from the estate agent with growing anger. She had just come home from work and had not even taken her coat off. Now she stood in her little kitchen, letter in hand and swore long and loud, using words she did not even know were in her vocabulary. Then she stormed out and went to rap on Zac's door.

'I've been expecting you, Mrs Bond.' He grinned at her.

She waved the letter at him. 'What do you make of this? Referring us to paragraph five of our tenancy agreement. What a nerve!'

'Take a deep breath and sit down. I'll make us a coffee or a tea if you prefer.' He went to switch on the kettle, then paused to look at her. 'I expect you haven't had anything to eat yet. Want to share my vegetable lasagna, it should be ready in ten minutes?'

As always, Zac's laid-back demeanour calmed her. 'Lasagna? Definitely yes.' She sank onto one of the kitchen chairs and put the letter down on the table. 'I know we've been expecting this, well sort of anyway, ever since Mrs Foley told us about those workmen that came into her shop and said they were surveying the house or whatever. I suppose I was trying not to believe it.'

Zac busied himself with setting the table and making two mugs of tea. He waited a few more minutes before he spoke. 'To be honest, the cottages could all do with a complete overhaul. I know we don't notice that any more, but not everyone wants a place where the front door opens right onto the kitchen. It would be nice to have a little hallway where you could hang up outdoor stuff. Bigger windows especially in the bedrooms. That kind of thing.'

'People have been living here for years, even their parents before them. We all belong here. Never mind the deficiencies. It's our home. I know we were all made to sign these tenancies a few years ago, just for the record according to the estate agent at the time. No one thought anything of it – and now this! People like Mad Bobby and Jimbo, where are they going to find a place they can afford? No, it's just not fair and I don't see why we should accept it.'

He placed plates of lasagna for them and then took the chair opposite. 'I know it's terrible and I'm with you all the way. But do you really think we can do anything about it?'

Sherry's chin jutted as she looked at him. 'You bet we can.'

CHAPTER THIRTY-TWO

Jessica was feeling very pleased with herself and with the world at large. She had managed to dodge Ross's calls. He had tried calling her three times already and had sent her a text which she had not yet answered: *Everything ok with you? Meet up this week?'* She had gone to the gym this morning for a workout -Samantha was absent again today to her relief. She had signed up for tai chi classes which were starting next week. She had then driven into the city and walked around the shops just to get in the mood for a romantic week away when Owen came home. And she had resisted the temptation to have even the tiniest drop of gin before she left the house.

The admission – if only to herself – that she was not trained for anything and would not be able to help out in Mrs Foley's shop even if she wanted to, nagged at the back of her mind. I'm intelligent, she thought, I'm not bad at maths, I can do the budgeting for myself and Owen. But still…

It was while she was passing an employment agency that she saw the card in the window: *Receptionist wanted for a boutique hotel*. Up until now, she had never considered looking for a job but today she felt buoyed up, enthusiastic about her life. She was pleased with herself that she had gone to the gym, and there was the romantic break with Owen to cheer her. At the back of her mind, she felt that when Owen came home this time, he would not go back to Africa. They could start looking for a nice house in a nice neighbourhood and she could leave the dark days of living in the cottage behind her. Until then it would be fun to go to work a few days a week. It would get her out of the house and give her the opportunity of meeting new people. Owen and the children would be both surprised and pleased, she knew.

The glamorous woman seated behind the desk in the employment agency, which was called Starlit Limited, eyed her approvingly, taking in her smart clothes and chic hairstyle, as she explained that she was interested in the advertised position as Receptionist at The Snow Queen hotel but did not have any of the usual papers – cv and references – with her.

'We really like people to apply online,' the Receptionist said with a smile that was about as genuine as a six-euro bank note. 'Can you tell me what experience of receptionist duties you have?'

Jessica was forced to admit that she had no actual experience working as a receptionist but she had hosted dinners with her husband in New York and London on several occasions and felt confident that she could meet and greet hotel guests.

The woman, whose badge proclaimed her to be Arquette, nodded and made a few notes on the pad in front of her. 'Any foreign languages?' she asked, flicking her blonde hair back out of her face.

'French, fairly fluent and a bit of Spanish.' Jessica produced her most charming smile, which was about as genuine as Arquette's had been. 'I've a few words in a lot of languages from travelling with my husband.'

Arquette nodded with what could have been approval. 'Could you take a seat and I'll just check with the hotel if anyone has time to see you today.'

Jessica sat down in one of the chairs in the corner of the room and Arquette proceeded to make the telephone call. Now that she was here, she hoped she might get the job. It would be fun to join the workforce after all these years. Sometimes when she had seen her neighbour Sherry arriving home from a busy day at the office, she had felt a bit envious. Yes, it was nice to have loads of leisure time now that the children had left home, but it was lonely too. Even if he came home, Owen would be out all day and knowing him would probably work late sometimes. It would be good to have a life of her own, so to speak. And she would prove something not only to herself but to her family.

She had arrived at this conclusion, when Arquette approached her. 'They can see you on Thursday afternoon around five o'clock, if you'd like,' she said.

Jessica's heart gave a little jump – a mixture of nerves and anticipation. Maybe this was the turnaround her life needed.

CHAPTER THIRTY-THREE

Millie checked her watch, which told her it was quarter to eight, nearly time to shut Mrs Foley's shop and go home. Mad Bobby and Jimbo were supposed to do the late shift tonight but they had not shown up. Although she knew neither of them was reliable, she had hoped that they would make an effort to fulfil their promise of helping in the shop. She guessed that Jimbo was having one of his drinking bouts and Mad Bobby was keeping a somewhat tipsy eye on him. Thank goodness Mrs Donovan was minding the twins. She began to tidy up. She counted the money in the till and entered the amount in the little ledger which Mrs Foley kept in a drawer of the counter. Customers had been few and far between after seven o'clock tonight. It probably wouldn't hurt to close early.

She had just completed the entry in the ledger, when a car drew up outside the shop. With a little sigh of annoyance - who was showing up shop so late, for goodness' sake, no home to go to? - she closed the till again and waited for the late comer to appear.

The sound of footsteps seemed very loud in the quietness and then to her surprise and displeasure, Jason DeVries appeared. She saw that he had clocked the downward turn of her mouth as he entered the shop.

'Sorry if I'm intruding,' he said, but without sounding very sorry.

Millie swallowed the anger which had welled up inside her. 'What can I do for you, Mr DeVries?'

She didn't know what she expected but it certainly was not his reply. 'I believe you are looking for a cat,' he said. 'I have it in my car and if you think it is Mrs Foley's, you can have it back.'

'Oh.' All she could do was gape at him.

'Do you want to check?' He gave the slightest of smiles, 'It's making a lot of noise. I'm surprised you haven't heard it from here.'

Millie came round the counter and preceded him out of the door to where his car was parked. He was right, you could hear the miaows of protest very clearly in the stillness.

DeVries opened the rear passenger door and showed her the cage with its furry protester. Yes, it was Daffodil. Relief swept over Millie. If it had been anybody else but DeVries she would have kissed him.

'Daffy, you're safe and sound.' There was a catch in her voice. 'Mrs Foley is going to be so happy.'

'Let's bring him inside then,' DeVries said. 'We don't want him to escape again, do we?'

He carried the cage into the shop and deposited it on the counter. Millie followed, taking care to shut the shop door firmly before releasing Daffy and hugging him. DeVries stood there watching her, not saying a word. After a few minutes she looked at him, recollecting her manners.

'Thank you, and thank you from Mrs Foley, she is going to be so relieved, she was very worried about him. He doesn't usually wander off like that. Where did you find him?' She knew she was babbling but could not stop. It was awkward thanking someone for a favour when you disliked them so much.

'He sometimes hung around that outhouse where you were looking for him the other day. I think another cat lives there so maybe he's fallen in love. Your children told me he'd come back so we went to get him.'

'My children?' She stared at him.

'Yes, they were playing around up in the yard and they told me they'd seen the cat. He seems to know them, so he let himself be caught. They're great kids,' he added with a smile at her which she did not return.

Millie had had no idea that Danny and Maeve played in the yard at Fernwood House. They did play outside after school but she had no idea they ventured that far. She would have to explain to them that Fernwood was off limits and let Mrs Donovan know, too. It was surprising that Jason had not said anything about it to her, considering he had warned her off so recently.

'Well, thank you again,' she said, trying to put some warmth into her voice. She expected him to leave now that he had returned the cat, but he remained standing there.

'You're working here now?'

'I'm helping out while Mrs Foley is in hospital. I've worked here once in a while when she needed someone to fill in, so I know the ropes.'

'You're doing it all on your own?' He sounded surprised.

Despite being grateful that he had found Daffy, Millie was finding it hard to be civil. She wanted him gone so that she could phone Mrs Foley and tell her the good news and then lock up the shop. What was it to him if she worked here twenty-four hours a day?

'All the neighbours are helping out as best they can,' she said quietly, stroking Daffy's head. 'That's what we do at Fernwood Cottages. We stick together.'

'I see. Well, if you need any help from me, let me know. I've moved into the big house for the time being.' Another of those faint smiles. 'You know where I live.'

'Thank you, that's very kind.'

He turned to go then but paused in the doorway. 'By the way, if you need a lift to see Mrs Foley in the hospital, please let me know. I'd be happy to drive you.' And without waiting for her reply, he left the shop.

It's much easier to hate someone if they are not being nice to you, Millie thought as she heard him drive away. But she refused to be back-footed. He had served notice on all the tenants here in Fernwood Cottages and nothing was ever going to change the way she felt about that or about him.

CHAPTER THIRTY-FOUR

'I've worked out a plan to upgrade Mrs Foley's shop,' Sherry told the little meeting which was held on the premises a few days after their first get-together on Sunday. They had agreed to meet up to see how they were managing and to fill any gaps which they might have missed. A few tweaks had been necessary: Mrs Donovan could not take Millie's twins on Fridays because she took turns visiting an old lady in the neighbourhood who was bedridden and needed her shopping done. Lady Moll had offered her services instead. Zac had agreed to come in early every Saturday to help take the various deliveries. Sherry had volunteered to work Sunday mornings. Mad Bobby said he could come in to help Zac and Jimbo had muttered something about 'being around' even though he had not specified what that meant. Both Jimbo and Mad Bobby had apologised for not showing up the other night to do the evening shift and promised it wouldn't happen again. Lady Moll gave a loud snort at this but refrained from making one of her cutting comments.

With these subjects out of the way, everyone was relaxing a little and Sherry made her announcement.

'If we want to fight the eviction orders, we need to draw attention to our little community here. We need to get the media interested in our story. For a start, I think we should make this shop the forefront of our campaign.' She looked around at the others who were watching her with noncommittal expressions. 'Let's do a bit of modernizing. Otherwise the general public will think it is perfectly all right to close the place down. But if we demonstrate how central to our little community the shop is and then expand on the effect the evictions would have, I think we'd get a lot of attention.'

'What have you in mind?' Lady Moll wanted to know. 'What do you mean exactly by "expand"?'

'I mean, first of all, we could install a coffee machine and start an advertising campaign, to draw in a bit of custom,' Sherry said. 'We could make sandwiches, too, and scones, so that people would pop in on their way to work. There's space for a few tables and chairs at the back of the shop, if you think about it so people could sit out in the summer. If we did a few posters, got the local papers interested in the story, we'd get more people involved. A lot of motorists use the main road on the way to the coast.'

'A bit risky, don't you think?' Lady Moll said. 'Supposing we don't get a return on the money we spend?'

'I'm not sure there is enough money to buy a coffee machine,' Millie said slowly. 'The shop has been making a loss, really, or at least just ticking along but I don't think there's enough money to invest in anything like that.'

'I've been talking to the people at The Haven Rescue,' Sherry told them. 'I think we could link promotion of the shop with promotion of the rescue centre. We could have a special sales day here in the shop with some of the proceeds going to The Haven. We'd get local radio and the local newspapers to cover that. You know, homemade cakes, maybe a raffle, things like that. I'm going to work out a programme which would benefit everyone.'

There were nods and murmurs from the others. Everyone was on board. Sherry gave a huge inward sigh of relief. Despite being worried about the future following the letter from the estate agent, they were all still determined to help out as much as they could.

Before parting, they agreed to meet again on Sunday morning. When nearly everyone had gone – only Zac and Millie remained – Sherry turned to Millie. 'Can we have a talk about finances, Millie?'

Millie nodded, looking relieved. She had probably thought her remark about the lack of money would be ignored, Sherry reckoned.

The two women and Zac sat down in the little kitchen at the back of the shop which Mrs Foley used for making herself a quick lunch.

'First things first, I think,' Sherry said when they had looked over the ledger and Millie had told them how much money - or how little to be precise - was on the shop's account at the bank. 'We'll do the fund-raising and depending on how much we can get, we'll do a little bit of modernising.'

'I'll have to clear it with Mrs Foley first,' Millie reminded her. 'I'll be seeing her tomorrow afternoon and I can talk to her about it. I haven't told her anything about the eviction notices. I don't want to upset her before her operation next week.'

Zac and Sherry nodded their agreement. 'We won't be doing anything drastic to the shop,' Sherry said. 'Just modernising it in a very small way. And if it brings in more turnover for her, it will be worth it.'

'If everyone volunteers for a few hours a week, Mrs Foley should manage the place comfortably enough when she's back on her feet,' Zac observed. 'She will need extra staff, though, if it does take off.'

'Very true,' Sherry nodded. 'But if it takes off as you put it, she'll be able to afford that. Looking at the accounts, I think she must worry a lot about surviving on so little income.'

'I think you're right,' Millie said. She knew Mrs Foley better than the others, having worked in the shop many times in the past. 'She seems so frail now, though, and who knows how she's going to be after the operation? If we're going to do anything, we have to make sure that we've covered all the angles so that she doesn't get overwhelmed with everything.'

'OK, let's see what I can come up with,' Sherry squared her shoulders. 'Whichever way we look at it, it will draw attention to the fact that tenants who have lived all their lives at Fernwood Cottages are being evicted including Mrs Foley herself. The shop would be a huge loss to the entire neighbourhood.'

'You have a lot on your plate already,' Zac reminded her later as the two of them walked back to his cottage. 'You have that report on setting up an office in Paris to finish, remember?'

'And I've been checking on what we can do about this eviction letter,' Sherry told him. 'I spoke to a solicitor and I'm going to see him on my way home from work tomorrow.'

They had reached Zac's cottage and he ushered her into the kitchen where he proceeded to make them both a coffee. He set down the mug of steaming liquid in front of her where she sat at the little table. 'Don't bite off more than you can chew,' he said. 'You can't do everything.'

She smiled at him. 'I know all that but I'm the only one who knows anything about marketing. I can't see Podge Donovan coming up with a master plan for the shop, can you?'

Zac had to laugh but then became serious again. 'It won't help anyone if you suffer a burn-out. Mike's going to have something to say about that.'

Sherry looked at him, hoping that she hid her surprise at the realization that tonight she had completely forgotten Mike and any claims he might have on her time.

CHAPTER THIRTY-FIVE

Jessica dressed carefully for her interview at The Snow Queen, opting for a skirt and matching jacket which looked businesslike. She had checked out the hotel's website. It was a medium-sized operation and according to its advertising was the trendiest place to stay at a reasonable price. She learned that the name The Snow Queen came from the name of the owners, William and Geoffrey Snow, something which had puzzled her. A name like that would be more appropriate for a ski resort location but perhaps it piqued the interest of tourists. The hotel had received lots of five-star reviews.

I should manage working at the Reception desk there, she told herself, as she applied mascara. After all, I'm sure I'm capable of welcoming guests and getting them checked in and taking reservations over the phone. She took another sip of gin and smiled at her reflection in the mirror. Yes, this could be the change in her life that she needed.

The hands of her watch seemed to creep until she deemed it time to get ready to drive into the city for her interview. She hesitated at the cottage door then turned back and poured herself another small measure of gin. It was only her third drink today. So what if it was Dutch courage? She wasn't really nervous, she told herself as brushed her teeth. She had nothing to prove after all and wasn't in dire need of a job. Still, it was a challenge, something completely new for her. She popped a piece of peppermint chewing gum into her mouth and made her way to her car which was parked in front of the cottage.

At The Snow Queen she was shown immediately into an office located behind the Reception area. She had just time to note that today the Receptionist on duty was very young and very made up, with improbably long eyelashes and bright red nails. I certainly won't come to work like that, she told herself.

The office was small and cramped with one tiny window. A plump grey-haired woman stood up to shake hands with her and invited her to be seated in the chair on the other side of the desk. She introduced herself as Trudie Koviac.

'Thank you for sending us your cv,' Trudie said. She looked down at the papers on her desk. 'It seems that you don't really have any experience in the hotel industry. Is that correct?'

'Well, no I don't, not exactly, but I've had a lot of experience in helping my husband organize and host business dinners and things like that.' Jessica produced her most engaging smile. 'He's a scientist and he often had to meet with investors and business people.'

Trudie's expression was impossible to read. 'Can you tell me why you think you would be the right person for the position as Receptionist?'

Was this the way job interviews usually went? Jessica sat up a bit straighter in her chair. For some reason she felt light-headed, that last shot of gin maybe wasn't such a good idea. 'I know what is expected of a Receptionist,' she said slowly,' I mean, how to make people feel welcome and all that. And I'm willing to learn.' This with the nicest smile she could muster.

Trudie looked down at the papers on her desk again. It seemed to Jessica that she had only just read the cv and letter of application which she had emailed yesterday. She finally closed the file and gave a brief nod.

'Thank you so much for taking the trouble to come and see us,' she said without sounding very thankful about it. 'I'm afraid we have been wasting your time. My assistant processed all the applications which is why I didn't realize that you have no experience in the hotel industry. We do need someone who can start with us fairly quickly but of course they would need to be experienced. We don't have time to train people in. I think this position is not for you. I'm sure you'll find something suitable in the near future.' She stood up and held out her hand. 'We appreciate your interest in The Snow Queen Hotel.'

Jessica walked out of the building towards where she had parked her car hardly aware of where she was going. She felt humiliated and stupid and naïve. What had made her think they would welcome her with open arms? Tears of disappointment, of mortification pricked her eyelids.

She slid into the driver's seat and sat very still for some minutes, staring through the windscreen without taking notice of what she was looking at. Her first thought was that she was glad she had not mentioned it to Owen. He would make light of the hotel's reaction, she knew. 'Not the end of the world Jess,' she could almost hear him saying it. He certainly would not understand how inadequate it made her feel not to be even remotely suitable to work behind a hotel reception desk.

The prospect of going home to her empty cottage and the vision of the long, lonely evening ahead was daunting. She had been looking forward to telling Owen about the new job, of hearing him voice approval and encouragement. And now, she was back to her role as the housewife, listening to her husband's business stories instead of having anecdotes of her own. She choked back a sob which was part frustration and part sadness.

Her phone beeped and she checked the incoming WhatsApp message. It was from Owen. *Hold off a bit on booking that holiday, Jess. Something's come up. I'll get back to you.*

Jessica felt as if she had been punched in the stomach. I'll bet he's not coming home in November like he promised, she thought. This was really the last straw. What was happening to her, to her marriage with Owen? Didn't he care how important that romantic trip away was to her? Was his business always to come first?

She lost track of how long she sat there until a quick check of the time told her that it was after six thirty. She did not want to go back to the emptiness of the cottage. For a few minutes she hesitated, then dialled Ross' number. Perhaps it was unfair, she would not be good company tonight, but she did need – oh how she needed – to feel that she was intelligent, capable, good fun. Ross' phone went to voicemail and she cut off without leaving a message, her hand shaking.

There was nothing else for it but to start the engine and drive home. Just as she came to this decision, her eye caught the lights of a little pub advertising hot food further down the street, reminding her that she was hungry. She had not eaten since breakfast, being too nervous about the interview at The Snow Queen. I'll have something to eat before I go home, she told herself. She blew her nose and checked her reflection in the mirror before getting out and locking the car. She stood for a moment, calling up the courage to go to a strange pub on her own, then turned and walked resolutely towards it. The place was nearly empty and she was able to take a seat by the open fire. They were serving evening meals the friendly barman assured her and brought her a menu.

'Something to drink?' he inquired when he had taken her order for beefburger and salad – there was not much choice on the menu.

Jessica hesitated then ordered a gin and tonic. One drink for the road would do no harm.

It was after nine o'clock when Jessica finally paid for her meal and the drinks. Where had the time gone? She walked slowly back to her car, feeling slightly unsteady on her feet. Surely I haven't had that much to drink? she asked herself. Admittedly, the barman had been very attentive, supplying her with wine and a final gin and tonic with her after-dinner coffee. Although the night air was cold and damp, she rolled the window on the driver's side down nearly all the way before setting off. A bit of fresh air would help her to sober up, she reckoned.

Traffic was light, much to her relief. She shook her head to clear it, gripping the wheel and concentrating hard. She had almost reached the turnoff for Loughborough Road which led to Greenfields shopping centre and which formed the last leg of her journey when a car swung out of a side street, headlights full on, blinding her. She braked hard, sending her vehicle into a spin before coming to a stop against a concrete pillar with a resounding crash, activating her airbag. Her foot was wedged between the brake and the accelerator and she felt pain dart through her whole body as she tried to move it. She sat for a few moments gasping for air before fighting her way out of the protecting folds of the airbag. Her hands were shaking as she put them up to cover her face, feeling a warm trickle of blood on her cheeks. She groped for the door lock only to find that the door had been badly dented and would not open.

She heard footsteps approaching. 'Are you all right?' a man's voice shouted at her through the open window of the car.

She turned to face him and recognition dawned. It was Zac, one of the residents at the cottages. 'Was – was it you? Did I –' She licked dry lips, her voice was hoarse, barely above a whisper. 'Did I hurt somebody?'

'No, it wasn't me. I've only just got here. Whoever it was, didn't wait,' Zac told her. 'You were going a fair lick,' he added.

So it's my fault, she thought.

'Come on,' Zac said, 'I'll help you out of the car. You'll have to get out by the passenger door, I'm afraid.'

He reached in and gently helped her slide over and out of the vehicle. She leant against the car, barely able to stand. Her whole body was shaking. She felt as if her ankle was broken.

The sound of sirens filled the air and the flashing blue lights told her that police and ambulances were on the scene. Her heart started to beat so fast that she thought she would suffocate.

One thing was frighteningly clear. She was going to be breathalysed and she was way over the limit.

CHAPTER THIRTY-SIX

'Here we are, Millie, ready to take over for you.'
Mad Bobby beamed at her as he and Jimbo walked into Mrs Foley's shop just after lunch. They had agreed at the last meeting that they would keep the place going while she visited Mrs Foley in the hospital. Zac had agreed to drive her there. She would be gone for only an hour or two and it was the quietest part of the day, and although she might have her misgivings about the two of them, she had no other choice.

'Thanks, guys,' she said. She went upstairs to get the bag she had packed with a change of clothes for Mrs Foley. Daffy was lying on the bed. He opened one eye as he heard her.

'Pity I can't smuggle you into the hospital,' she told him. 'Mrs Foley really misses you.'

He yawned, showing a pink tongue.

She was just emerging from the shop, expecting to see Zac waiting for her, when a familiar car slid to a stop in front of her. Jason DeVries got out from behind the wheel and held the passenger door open for her.

'Zac sends his apologies,' he said. 'I met him at Whiddys garage when I was collecting my car. He can't drive you today so he asked if I could do it and of course I'm only too happy to help.'

Jason DeVries was the last, the very last person she wanted to be obliged to. She knew she should have been grateful to him for finding Daffy and for giving her a lift to the hospital, but she could not forget that he was responsible for evicting everyone at Fernwood Cottages. Only the thought of Mrs Foley, who was expecting her today, made her meekly slip into the passenger seat.

'Has something happened to Zac?' She asked as they set off.

'One of your neighbours had an accident last night. Jessica something-or-other. I gather she damaged her car. He was at Whiddy's sorting things out for her. He mentioned something about her husband being abroad.'

'That would be Jessica Clifford. Was she hurt?'

'Not badly hurt, he said, a sprained ankle and some bruising if I understood correctly. Do you know her?'

'Not really, just to say hello. She keeps herself to herself. I'll call on her today on my way home to see if she needs anything.'

He gave a quick glance in her direction before returning his attention to the road. 'You all pitch in to help, even for people you barely know?'

Millie shrugged. 'Zac helps everyone around here. Most of the people in Fernwood Cottages are old and don't have family living close to them. Zac does all the odd jobs for them. It's no problem for me to pick up a few groceries on my way home.'

'I believe you do everyone's shopping?'

Now who had told him that? Gossipy Mrs Donovan, no doubt.

'Just for Jimbo and Mad Bobby. Neighbours are neighbours. They'd do the same for me if I needed. That is what living in a community means and who knows how much longer we are all going to be allowed live here.' She was surprised at herself, at her courage in saying what she thought. From her years with Kevin, she had learned to keep her mouth firmly shut.

He turned his head to give her another of those looks. 'I can't pretend not to understand where you're coming from, but I don't think this is either the time or the place to discuss the matter.'

She made no reply and they were both silent until they reached the hospital.

'I'll be waiting for you in the car park when you've finished visiting,' he said as she got out of the car.

Millie would have dearly loved to tell him that she could make her own way home, thank you very much, but she did need a lift and therefore mumbled her thanks before heading towards the main hospital entrance.

CHAPTER THIRTY-SEVEN

'Have you finished the proposal for Piers?' Vicky stopped by Sherry's desk to ask the question, her eyes taking in what Sherry was wearing today. 'I love that jacket,' she added. 'Is it new? Don't remember seeing it before.'

'This? Not new. I haven't worn it in yonks.' Sherry waved a dismissive hand. Truth be told, she had plucked it out of her wardrobe in a hurry this morning, having overslept. She had worked very hard last night on her plan for Mrs Foley's shop, having first stopped by The Haven on her way home to go through their accounts with Sally, the Haven's treasurer. The concert had brought in much needed funds and a decision had to be reached how to spend them wisely. Although it was late when she got home, she turned to her draft on Mrs Foley's shop. Her plan had occupied her thoughts as she had gone through the day. Once or twice she had to force herself to concentrate on the tasks in hand. When she got home, she had heated a mug of soup, buttered a slice of toast and then sat down at her laptop to continue with the marketing plan. She had not even glanced at the draft proposal for Piers Halloran.

'I've just handed in my proposal to Piers,' Vicky said, 'he asked me if I knew when yours would be ready.'

Sherry forced a smile, even though she was mentally gritting her teeth. 'I'm working on it. Piers will get the report in good time. It's not due until the beginning of next week.'

Lately, she found herself tempted to take the job if the proposal was successful. The challenge involved in setting up an office appealed to her. What would Mike's reaction be? That was the problem. When she was in a positive mood, she felt that he would beg her not to go, that this would make him realize that they needed each other, needed to get married. But on bad days, she saw herself alone and lonely in Paris with occasional visits from Mike dwindling slowly to nothing.

'Just thought I'd tell you that I've handed in my proposal.' Vicky still hovered at her desk. 'What are you doing for the weekend? I expect you and Mike are going to this new play that's opening in the Artists Centre? Dinner and culture they said on FaceBook. Sounds fun.'

'We haven't made any plans as yet.' Sherry turned pointedly to her computer. 'I'd better get on. I have a meeting in about an hour and I need to do some background work.'

Vicky stood a moment longer, looking over Sherry's shoulder in the hopes of getting a glimpse of what she was working on. It would not be the first time that Vicky had stolen an idea and passed it off as her own.

'Want to go to lunch?' she asked. 'The girls said they're going to Sam's Place at around one o'clock.'

Sam's Place was a small pub not far from the office, a favourite dining place with the staff. Sherry sometimes joined them there but of late she avoided it. She was getting more and more sensitive about her relationship with Mike which was not only due to Vicky's curiosity and nosy questions. Her colleagues were expecting her to announce her engagement to

Mike any day, especially since her sister's recent engagement. Would he propose at Christmas? The more she obsessed about it, the less hopeful she was. Yes, they were happy as they were, as he so often said – or were they? When she sat in the pub, she sometimes looked around at her married colleagues. They were all ordinary women, not super glamorous, not super clever or successful. But they had husbands who cared about them, they had children who they were proud of, and though they might moan about the struggle to meet the mortgage or how the kids were doing at school, they were all in a committed relationship. If there was some magical ingredient to this, Sherry could not discover it in their faces.

Vicky was waiting for an answer. Breakfast had been a quick slug of coffee this morning and the day was long. Sherry nodded. 'Yes, I'll be there. See you then.'

Sherry joined the others at Sam's Place and ordered a chicken salad and a non-alcoholic beer. Her meeting with clients Mulavanny & Co, a small meat processing business, had gone well. The company wanted to expand and she was requested to draw up plans for this new venture. It was a challenge and she would need to work late tonight to satisfy her client's requirements.

'Hey Sherry,' one of her colleagues whose name was JJ, called her attention across the little group around the table. 'Piers has been talking very highly of you, I hear. He's expecting great things. You're one of the best.' He grinned at her and the others laughed and clapped "well done, Sherry.".

Sherry stole a side glance at Vicky whose mouth had taken a pronounced downturn, although she had joined in the clapping. When her eyes met Sherry's, they were glistening with what could only be classified as jealousy. 'I'm sure Mike won't let you wander off to foreign parts,' she said sweetly.

Somehow she guessed that all between Mike and Sherry was not idyllic and occasionally made some snide remark which Sherry always ignored, although she felt the barb despite trying to ignore it.

Sherry merely smiled and began to tuck into her salad. Her other colleagues looked uncomfortable for a moment, before someone changed the subject. They probably discuss me and Mike behind my back, Sherry thought to herself while trying to appear unconcerned. Office gossip. But then if it was one of them, I'd do the same she acknowledged. She let the conversation flow around her, feeling hurt and humiliated and angry at Mike as the cause of it. It was mostly light-hearted stuff, a few moans about their boss, Piers, and a few stories on kids in school and how crazy one of the maths teachers was. She was glad that she did not need to do more than laugh at the appropriate intervals. Would she ever be in a position to join in, to relate some amusing story of her own family? Of late, she was seriously beginning to doubt this. And again she asked herself, was moving to Paris the answer?

CHAPTER THIRTY-EIGHT

Jessica sat huddled in her dressing gown, drinking a black coffee and trying to come to terms with what had happened last night. She would lose her driving licence, at least for a bit, that much was certain. Repairs to the car would be costly, although that was minor compared to a driving ban. Zac had arranged for the car to be towed to a garage and promised to help her with getting it sorted. Meanwhile she was stranded here at Fernwood Cottages with a badly sprained ankle. Zac had loaned her a walking stick. She was not sure what she would have done without his help last night.

One thing was for sure, she would have to appear in court. Everyone would find out about it, including Alicia and Samantha and Ross would get to know what had happened. Her cheeks burned at the thought. She had managed to keep Ross at a distance over the past week or so, inventing excuses for not seeing him. What would he think of her now? And whatever she told herself to the contrary, she did not want him to think less of her for drink driving.

Her mobile phone interrupted her gloomy thoughts. She had not heard from Owen since his message last night about putting the holiday booking on hold. When he did ring her, she would have to tell him about the accident with the car, although she would not reveal that she had had too much to drink and would most likely lose her driving licence at least for a short while.

When she checked, she saw that the caller was her son Noah. She spoke to her children once a week, usually on Saturday afternoons, so this call was unexpected.

'Is everything all right?' She asked when the usual greetings were over.

'Everything's fine,' he assured her. 'I'm calling about Halloween. You're coming over, right?'

'That's the plan. I'm looking forward to seeing you and Selena.'

'Yeah, I know. Only. Look, mum, Selena and I have been invited to spend Halloween in the Lake District. It's actually for a good cause, a local charity here, for the homeless, you know? We've been asked to take part in a spooky event in a big old house near Keswick belonging to one of the professors. There's about twenty of us going to put on a show. It'll be great fun.'

Both Noah and Selena were interested in amateur dramatics, as Jessica knew. Normally she would have been delighted for them and very proud that they were asked to participate in something like that. She could not speak for a minute or two as she digested Noah's news. First there was Selena not coming home for Christmas and now both of them not available at Halloween.

'You don't mind?' Noah asked. 'I think you said that you hadn't booked a flight yet. Maybe we can meet up later. And anyway I'll be home for Christmas.'

'No. No. I don't mind. I was going to book my flight today so it's just as well you told me now. You go ahead. I'm – I'm very pleased, proud of you both. Your dad will be, too.'

'Like I said, we can meet up after Halloween. Nothing to stop you and dad coming over for a long weekend then, is there?' He sounded relieved – had he really expected her to object?

'Of course. You have a good time. I expect you'll need some extra money?' That's probably why he phoned, she thought sadly.

'Well, yeah, that would be good, mum. We don't need a lot, just a bit to help pay for the costumes and that. All for a good cause.'

'Yes,' she said dully. 'No problem. I'll arrange a bank transfer. Let me know how much you're likely to need.'

When she had finished the call, she cried quietly, her face buried in her hands. After what seemed a very long time, she roused herself, showered and dressed and then called Owen's number. She desperately needed to know why he had asked her to put the booking of their romantic weekend on hold.

Owen's phone went to voicemail but he called her back within ten minutes. 'Something wrong, Jess? I'm very tied up in a meeting.'

He was always tied up, she thought suddenly. She was always the one with nothing to do, nothing waiting for her. Unemployable. The word formed in her head and although she knew it was a direct result of not getting the job at The Snow Queen, it made her feel even more useless than ever.

'You said in your text that I should hold off on booking our week in November.'

'Sorry about that. I think I've got it sorted now, though, and I should make it. Have you checked out hotels already?'

'I just need you give me firm dates for when you're coming home.'

'I'll have to get back to you. Promise. What else has been going on?'

He probably guessed from her voice that she was feeling down, she thought.

'Noah rang me to say that he and Selena won't be in Edinburgh for Halloween. They're doing some kind of spooky show in Keswick in the Lake District for a homeless charity, organized by one of their professors, I believe, so I won't go over there as I'd planned. Just as well he told me today as I was going to book my flight and hotel.'

'All right. It's not the end of the world, Jess. I know you were looking forward to seeing them but we'll all get-together soon. We can spend a weekend in Edinburgh with them before Christmas, seeing as how Selena will be away for the festive season. That all? I have to get back to my meeting.'

'The tenants in the cottages are planning some kind of resistance to those termination notices I told you about,' she said. 'We're not affected, are we? I mean the cottage belonged to your family for ages, didn't it?'

'Nothing to worry about,' he said in a reassuring tone. 'At least not from our point of view. But I'm sorry for the people there. They're the salt of the earth. What are they planning?'

'I don't know. I haven't been involved.'

'I think you should just show up, Jess. After all, they are neighbours. Where do they meet?'

'Mrs Foley's shop. I'm not sure I can contribute anything. Sherry is a very capable woman.'

'Still, I think you ought to put in an appearance.'

Jessica pursed her lips. She did not agree with him, but she knew, as most husbands and wives know, that he would nag her to death if she did not attend at least one meeting. Well, what had she to lose, really? Without her car, she would not be going anywhere, in any case.

'All right,' she said. 'I'll pop into the next get-together and see how they're doing.'

'Great.' She could tell he was smiling. 'Look, I really have to go, Jess. Love you.'

And then he was gone. She felt happier now that the prospect of that romantic weekend had been restored, although a doubt lingered if he really would be home for it. She knew she should have told him about the accident with the car, but she just could not face up to it at this moment. He would be really angry with her if he knew she had been drinking and driving.

Later that evening the doorbell rang when she had settled herself down with a double shot of gin and tonic. Her neighbour Millie stood on the doorstep.

'I heard about the accident,' she said, 'I can do your shopping if you need anything.'

Jessica was both touched and irritated. Her head was swimming from too many gins and tonic today.

'That's really kind. I'll let you know. Right now, I don't need anything.' She hoped that she sounded both sober and thankful.

Millie was looking at her curiously. 'No trouble,' she said before taking leave.

Jessica hobbled into the bathroom and studied her face in the mirror over the basin. Yes, she did look rough, her eyes were bloodshot. Hopefully Millie would put this down to the accident.

Everyone was being so kind, she reflected, well at least Zac and Millie were. No doubt nosy Mrs Donovan would poke her head in tomorrow to get all the details of the accident. Am I being an ungrateful bitch? She asked her reflection.

CHAPTER THIRTY-NINE

'I'm afraid the tenancy agreements are pretty water-tight,' Walter Dunne the solicitor looked at Sherry over the top of his reading glasses. 'They were revised and updated around seven years ago. Everyone signed.'

'I think I have the latest version. I gave you a copy.' Sherry indicated the papers on his desk. 'Does this mean that we have no earthly hope of getting the termination notices annulled?'

Dunne flicked the pages on his desk with his fingers. 'They're pretty water-tight,' he repeated. 'I think the idea was to set everything up for Mr Hatton's heirs.'

'I believe Jessica Clifford owns the cottage she lives in, or at least her husband does. Supposing they want to stay? Would that have any effect on Jason DeVries' plans?'

Dunne shrugged. 'I'm sure that if a suitable offer was made, the Cliffords would be happy to sell to the new owners. Either way, it wouldn't have any influence on the plans for the cottages, I wouldn't think.'

Sherry mulled this over for a minute or two. 'Supposing we were to find enough funds to buy all the cottages ourselves. Do you think we'd have a chance of staying on?'

'Money will buy you most things.' Dunne gave a thin-lipped smile. 'I doubt though that your neighbours have the wherewithal, at least that is what I gathered from you when we discussed this on the phone.'

'If we could raise the money from somewhere, or even half of it, it would be a start,' Sherry said slowly, her mind already turning over possibilities. 'But I mustn't keep you,' she added, mindful of solicitor's fees.

Dunne stood up immediately. 'One thing,' he said as he held open his office door for her. 'Strictly off the record: If you decide to fight this, it will be a costly business and my gut feeling is that you would lose.'

'That's about the size of it,' Sherry said, addressing the meeting of the cottage tenants next evening. She had just given them a run down on what Walter Dunne had said, including the bit about any attempt to fight it being costly and probably doomed to fail.

They were crammed into Mrs Foley's shop, this now being the unofficial meeting place. Sherry was surprised to see that Jessica Clifford was among those present. She had hobbled here with the help of the walking stick Zac had given her.

'What do you think we should do?' The question came from Mad Bobby. 'We'll never find anywhere like this that we can afford.'

'And what about Mrs Foley?' Jimbo looked at Millie. 'What's she supposed to do, poor woman?'

'She's over her operation,' Millie said. 'I haven't spoken to her about all this because she's really not fit enough. There were some complications to that fracture. They're going to keep her in the hospital for another couple of days. After that she'll have to go to a nursing home for a bit until she's able to take care of herself.'

'I'm sure that she'll agree to whatever we decide,' Sherry said.

There was a general nodding of heads and everyone started talking together.

'I've been thinking,' Sherry interrupted. 'We have a few options.'

She had their attention now. 'We can try buying the cottages, everyone puts in their savings and we'd have to fund-raise as well.'

'Do you think DeVries would agree to that?' Jimbo asked. He was not normally so talkative or so sober. 'Have we any idea about how much money we're talking about?'

'I've no idea.' Sherry confessed. 'We have to get the cottages evaluated.' She looked at Jessica Clifford. 'You own your cottage, Jessica. Have you any idea how much it's worth?'

Jessica started at being addressed. 'I have no idea,' she said. 'I'd have to ask my husband.'

'There is another option, or at least an idea,' Sherry said. 'We can get the local media and maybe even national media interested in the case. I'll write up a piece about the hardship for the tenants and how you've all been living here so long. That might get attention. If anyone knows a politician who'd get involved, we should try that as well.' She looked around at them all. 'We could try organizing a demonstration at the Big House and have the media cover it.'

Again, there were murmurs of agreement. If she were honest, Sherry was not convinced that they could summon up enough protestors to make a good story for the media but it would be worth a try. She was even more doubtful that they could find enough demonstrators to show up at Fernwood House to make an impression either on Jason DeVries or even the local newspaper.

'Why don't we talk to DeVries?' Mrs Donovan said. 'Nobody has approached him as far as I know.' She looked at

Millie. 'He's given you a lift a few times, Millie. Did he ever mention this business to you?'

Millie shook her head. 'No. he didn't. We never have much to say to each other. I've never brought it up,' she added, flushing slightly as all eyes turned on her. 'I didn't know what to say to him, really.'

'Actually, I bumped into him in town yesterday,' Sherry said. 'I suggested to him that we meet up for a coffee and he promised to get in touch. He has my phone number.' She looked at Millie. 'It might be an idea if you come with me. At least he knows who you are and let's be honest, he has been obliging in driving you to see Mrs Foley. Maybe he's a lamb in wolf's clothing after all.'

'Are you sure you want to go through with all this?' Zac asked later as he and Sherry were having a very late supper at his cottage. Zac could rustle up a tasty meal in no time from whatever was in his store cupboard. He had not attended the meeting this evening, pleading some odd jobs in the neighbourhood that needed to be done, and she had just filled him in on everything that was said and agreed on.

Sherry looked at him in surprise. This was not like the Zac she knew. Yes, he was pretty laid back about most things but not about perceived injustices. He had campaigned with her two years ago to get a better bus service for the area.

'Yes, of course I want to go through with it,' she said. 'We have to put up a fight and we might even win if we get enough public interest in it.'

'Supposing DeVries agreed to pay everyone a good sum of money to help them find a new place to live?'

'A good sum of money? Money isn't the answer here, Zac. Don't you understand? The cottages are home to most of the tenants. I know I'm not here that long in comparison but I love the place. And besides, you're forgetting Mrs Foley. What is she supposed to do with the shop?'

Before he could make any reply, her phone beeped. It was Mike.

'Sorry I couldn't make it tonight,' he said cheerfully. 'What are you doing with yourself? Did you go to this protest meeting?'

For a second or two, Sherry's mind went blank. 'Yes, I did,' she said after half a minute, 'and it's not a protest meeting. We're trying to find ways to fight back.'

'Good luck with that.'

Zac was watching her, his expression hard to read. She pulled a face at him as a form of apology for taking the call.

'Mike, do you know anyone in the media who might want to campaign for us, or even report on what's happening here at Fernwood Cottages? We could use some publicity.'

'Stories like that are ten a penny. Look, I've got to go, I promised Al and Jill I'd drop them home tonight. I just wanted to know if there was anything new on the tenancies front. Talk tomorrow, OK? Love you, Sherry.'

'I'd better go home,' she said to Zac when she and Mike had said their goodnights. 'I've got a long day tomorrow and old Piers is waiting for my proposal on this new venture of his.'

Only when she closed her cottage door behind her, did she realize that it had again slipped her mind that Mike was supposed to come over tonight.

CHAPTER FORTY

The last thing Millie expected was to be seated opposite Jason DeVries and Sherry in The Corner Café in Greenfields shopping centre. Jason had ordered lattes for them and they waited until the waitress had served them before broaching the subject of their meeting.

'You can guess why we want to talk to you,' Sherry said after she had taken a sip of her latte. 'We are all shocked and worried by the notice to quit our cottages. We'd like to get your side of the story on that, please.'

Jason had the grace to look uncomfortable. He played with his coffee spoon, not looking directly at either of them.

'It's a long story,' he said. 'The DeVries family are indirectly related to the Hatton family who owned Fernwood House. Many years ago, one of the DeVries ladies had a child with one of the Hattons, Benjamin Hatton to be exact. She was visiting cousins or something, I'm not clear on the details. They never married and in those days everything was hushed up. Her name was Grace DeVries. She was sent off to live in Australia and no one heard anything about her.'

'An old, old story,' Sherry observed.

Millie said nothing. She wondered if he was trying to get their sympathy by this recital of family history.

'Anyway,' Jason went on after a minute or two, 'to get to the point. It seems that Benjamin's grandfather or grandmother – I'm not sure which – traced the child in Australia and kept in touch with Grace and her son who she called Ben after his father. When old Mr Hatton died, it was discovered that he had left Fernwood House and estate to Ben. As you know, he never married and in fact he was not directly related to Benjamin Hatton. He left a letter to say that he felt that Alice DeVries had been treated very unfairly, a disgrace to the Hatton name, and he wanted to make up for it. However, Ben had himself died some years previously. He'd never married either and had no known heirs.

'That's all a bit sad,' Sherry said. 'We all knew that Stanley Hatton was an oddity. He kept to himself mostly but he was a good landlord. He never raised our rents.'

Jason glanced at her and then at Millie, his expression not giving anything away. 'I have only met Stanley twice in my life, once when I was here on a holiday and once when I did some business for the family in Dublin and came here to visit him, but for some reason he had arranged that if Ben Hatton or his heirs could not be traced, I was to inherit Fernwood House. So here I am.'

There was a short silence while they absorbed this information. Rumour had suggested that the DeVries family had purchased the Fernwood estate.

'That's all very interesting and would make a good story in the media,' Sherry said slowly. 'However, it's not helping us one little bit. Why can't everything go on as before? You could let out the land and leave us all in peace.' She hesitated before adding, 'I imagine that you have a career or a business of your own.'

'To be honest, I didn't know what to think when I was told that I'd inherited the place,' Jason confessed. 'Bradfords, my estate agent, who have been dealing with renting the place out for years, have told me that a few people are interested in buying it with a view to converting the house into a hotel and the cottages into holiday homes. I have no ties in Ireland so at present that seems to be the best solution.'

This calm statement made Milly find her voice, surprising both herself and her two companions. 'Can you imagine what it means to the tenants of the cottages to be evicted after living here most of their lives?'

'Look, as I said, it seems to be the best solution. A hotel located here would mean jobs for the area, for one thing.'

She glared at him. 'Fernwood estate has been lying idle for years. All the land has been rented out to local farmers. Old Mr Hatton was happy with that. You must have known that old Mr Hatton wouldn't live forever and that changes were bound to happen. Fernwood House hasn't cost you a penny really, seeing as how you inherited everything.'

'I can't help the fact that I inherited the place. I knew nothing about it until a month or so ago.'

'And we all lose our homes, just like that,' Millie went on as if he had not spoken. 'No one even thought of consulting us.' She glanced in Sherry's direction for moral support, but Sherry said nothing.

'How long have you been renting your cottage?' Jason asked.

'I came here about five years ago with the children to get away from an abusive partner. The rent was cheap and I have very little money. But it's not about me. Other tenants have lived here all their lives. Take Mad Bobby or Jimbo, they have very little income. Families with eight or nine children all lived in those little cottages and worked on the estate. They felt they belonged. And now they're being asked to leave.'

'You're all very united, aren't you,' Jason spoke slowly as if turning over what she had said in his mind. 'I've never come across that in my entire life, the way you all hang together.'

'We depend on each other. We're neighbours. I've been very lucky that I was accepted from the start as one of their own. That is not something you find in the big cities. Maybe we'll never find it again.'

Sherry had brought her along as back-up so why wasn't she saying a word? She cast a sidelong glance in Sherry's direction and found that she was looking from Jason to herself but with apparently no intention of interjecting a comment.

Jason gave a faint sigh. 'Look, I know you all think I'm the bad guy and I don't blame you. We'll try and help you with finding a place to live. Our estate agent should know of a few places that would be suitable and surely the local councils can help?'

Millie said nothing. He would find out soon enough that renting was an expensive business even for people with good jobs. There were long waiting lists for council housing. With her two children, she had a reasonable chance of getting some kind of accommodation but for the others it would be a problem. It did not seem worthwhile to try and explain this to him.

'It's not only moving somewhere else,' she said to break the silence that followed his last remark. 'These are their homes, where they want to live out their lives. Everyone needs a place to belong and they belong here at Fernwood Cottages. And then you come along and chuck them out onto the street without a thought.'

'I'm sorry, I can't see what else I can do.' He did sound as if he meant it. But what was the use of that?

They stood up and Sherry excused herself to go to the rest rooms. When she had gone, Jason turned to Millie.

'I really am sorry. I know you don't believe me but I am. I think you're a really brave woman, Millie.'

It was the first time that he had used her Christian name. She looked at him in surprise. There was a something, she did not know what to call it, in his tone of voice that caused a tiny flutter in the pit of her stomach.

'If you need a lift to visit Mrs Foley at any time, please let me know,' he said quietly. 'I'd be happy to help.'

She was saved having to answer by Sherry's arrival back from the restrooms.

'You were great, Millie, I think you really got through to him, much better than I could have,' Sherry said later as she drove them home. 'At least now he has some idea of what his plans will mean to his tenants.'

Millie thought back to Jason's words and use of her first name and then deliberately stopped thinking about it.

'I doubt if it will make much difference,' was all she said.

CHAPTER FORTY-ONE

The damage to her car was more extensive than Jessica had anticipated. The workshop phoned her to say that they would try and get it sorted by the end of next week. She had also caused some damage to the pillar she had crashed into and she would have to pay for that, as the letter from the local council informed her this morning. Right now, she did not care one way or the other. Together with the letter from the council, she had received a summons to appear before the District Court on Monday week. She dreaded the idea. She had never had a brush with the law before now. Should she get a solicitor? What if someone she knew saw her, or heard about it all? Jessica Clifford in court on a drink driving charge! She cringed inwardly. Nosy Mrs Donovan would make the most of that. The gossips would be delighted. Owen would be furious when he found out.

While he was at home, she had never had too much to drink, nor even been tempted to drink gin at night as she did at present. And she had certainly never consumed alcohol if she was driving. She knew that it was her way of coping with the loneliness of Owen and the children being away. She needed something to fill up her days. But was drinking gin the answer? What was becoming of her? She hobbled up and down in the little kitchen-cum-living room. How long would she be disqualified for? She had heard somewhere that it depended on how much alcohol was in your system. But even three months without her licence would be inconvenient, a disaster if she were honest. The cottage was so isolated unless you had your own car. And Owen would find out when – if - he came home in November. He would be so upset with her.

A knock at the door interrupted her restless pacing. She looked out of the window but from here could not see who the caller was. I hope it's not Mrs Donovan, she thought, if it is I just won't answer. She'll have noticed that my car isn't parked outside and by now she'll probably have heard about the crash. Wait until she hears about the drink driving and losing my licence! She'll make a meal of that. You couldn't keep anything secret in this area.

There was another rap on the door. To her surprise, and relief, she found Ross standing on the doorstep.

'Hi there, gorgeous.' He gave her a big smile. Then as she hesitated, he added 'aren't you going to invite me in?'

She opened the door wide without a word and he walked into the kitchen and turned to face her. 'Is everything all right? I see that you're limping. I heard you had a bash with your car. Why didn't you tell me? What's going on? Have I done something to annoy you? If I have, you only have to say.'

She had not seen him for over a week. Her heart started to thump and she felt the colour rising to her cheeks. She was behaving like a teenager with her first crush, she knew, feeling foolish but somehow excited to see him, too.

She had done her best to keep him at bay, texting him just once to say that at the moment she could not meet with him for various reasons, which she did not specify.

And now she was being pulled into the full force of his charm. He did seem to really like her. But no, she refused to go down that road. She would never dream of cheating on Owen.

'It's nothing like that,' she told him. 'I've just been busy lately.' She was conscious all of a sudden how she must look. She was not wearing make-up, her hair was all over the place and the jeans and sweatshirt she was wearing, if not shabby, were anything but glamorous.

'I missed you,' he said. 'I hope you don't mind my dropping in like this. I just wanted to hear your voice, to see you again.'

'Ross, please remember that I'm married,' she said, not looking at him. 'We can ever only be friends.'

He spread his hands palms upward in a gesture of surrender. 'I know. I know. We can be friends and still see each other and have a good time. Don't you agree?'

'Yes, but –'

'So you'll come out with me for a bite to eat today?'

Suddenly she wanted very much to go for a meal with him, to sit and talk and laugh and forget the car crash and the impending drink driving charge and the failure to get that job at The Snow Queen. She felt he would understand, would not judge her for drinking and driving. And she wanted very much to have support and understanding and not hear a lecture on road safety.

'All right,' she said, and found she was smiling. 'You win.'

'Wonderful. Just what I need.' He looked as if he really meant it.

'Give me a few minutes to get ready?'

'Sure.' He pulled out a chair and sat down.

She went into the bedroom and hastily changed into her favourite Ralph Lauren olive trousers and floral jumper. She brushed her hair, applied make up and added a splash of Baccarat Rouge 540. Owen had given her the scent for

Christmas last year and she regretted immediately that she had used it now when going out with Ross, even if it was not really "going out", as she hastily amended to herself. It was simply her favourite scent and surely there was no need to overthink using it? She turned away from the mirror. What she needed now was a shot of gin to lift her spirits, help her relax, make her good company for the evening. Although tempted this morning, she had not taken a drink yet today. The only trouble was that Ross was sitting in the kitchen and she kept the bottle of gin in a cupboard there. He would notice if she took out the gin bottle.

When she returned to the kitchen, Ross was scrolling through his mobile. She hobbled to the cupboard as quickly as she could, hoping he would remain engrossed in his scrolling. She half opened the door, her hand reaching for the gin bottle. She had placed her body in the way so that he would not be able to see what she was doing. She unscrewed the cap of the bottle and drank in three big gulps, feeling the reassuring sting as the gin went down, then retreated to the bathroom to brush her teeth. Hopefully Ross would not smell the alcohol on her breath.

'You are so beautiful,' he said when she reappeared in the kitchen. 'Please, don't ever disappear on me again.'

CHAPTER FORTY-TWO

'They've found a nursing home for me,' Mrs Foley said when Millie next visited her. 'I'll be there for a bit, they said. They found a few things wrong with me. Mind you, I couldn't tell you what they are. I don't understand all that medical talk.' Her smile was a faint imitation of her happier days when she had bustled about the shop full of energy.

'That's good news,' Millie said. 'Where is the nursing home? Not too far away, I hope?'

'It's a posh place, The Laurels it's called, they said it's private. I think my sister must have organized it. I couldn't afford it anyway. I don't know how she can either, really.'

'You deserve it'. Millie reached out and took both the other woman's hands in hers.

'How are you managing with the shop?' Lines of worry creased the older woman's forehead. 'I hope you're all right with the money. You have a family to look after. You can take out what you need from my bank account.'

Millie did not have the heart to tell her that when deliveries had been paid for, there would scarcely be enough money in the bank. Mrs Foley had savings, she knew, but she did not want to touch them. There would almost certainly be hospital and doctors' bills to be paid. The thin trickle of customers meant that there was not much money coming in at the moment. Although she still went to clean for Alicia Scott-Douglas twice a week, Millie had had to scale back some of her cleaning jobs and was under severe financial strain. Alicia Scott-Douglas had surprisingly come up trumps, assuring Millie that she could pick what hours suited her to come and clean during the week. People could really surprise you, Millie thought.

'Mrs Foley thinks her sister is paying for the nursing home,' Millie told Zac as he drove her home. 'She's not sure how her sister is managing to do that because she doesn't have much money of her own. I think she's very worried about everything. It's not helping her recovery.'

'What about you?' Zac inquired. 'Have you got enough money to manage? I don't suppose you can juggle your cleaning jobs and the shop.'

'I still do some cleaning. Mrs Donovan is helping look after the children, she brings them to and from school while I'm at Alicia Scott-Douglas's place in the evenings. I really appreciate Alicia letting me change my hours. Mrs Donovan has been been marvelous but now and then she sort of says she can't do this forever and I don't blame her. The other cleaning jobs I had are on hold, they are most likely gone to someone else by now. I mean, people need their cleaning done regularly.'

'You do nearly a full day in the shop, don't you?'

'Well, yes. There isn't anyone else. Jimbo and Mad Bobby do come in for a couple of hours here and there but there's no one else and on what she takes in, Mrs Foley couldn't afford to hire someone.'

Zac never said a great deal and she knew that she could trust him, that whatever she told him would be kept to himself.

'What about our new neighbour Jessica Clifford?' he asked after a little pause in the conversation. 'She came to the last meeting at the shop or so Sherry tells me.'

'Yes but she didn't really have anything to say. I think she was just curious to see what was going on at the meetings. Besides, she sprained her ankle so she's not able to get about very well.'

'She needn't do a lot of walking, just sit behind the counter. Might be an idea to ask her if she'd help out on one or two mornings. That would leave you free to take up at least one other cleaning job while the kids are at school. She might even be looking for a cleaner herself. I can't see her scrubbing out the kitchen, somehow.'

'I don't know,' Millie said doubtfully. 'I'll think about that.' She was not sure that she wanted to approach Jessica, who seemed to look down on the other residents of Fernwood Cottages. But maybe I'm being unfair, she chided herself. All the same, she doubted that she would ever risk asking the other woman and getting a humiliating snub.

CHAPTER FORTY-THREE

'Sherry, can you come into my office a minute, please?' Piers asked, sounding very uptight.

It was almost lunchtime and Sherry had decided to get a sandwich from the deli and work through it. She was way behind on the business plan for Williams & Williams, a software accessory company who were launching a new product. Come what may, she had to get this done today.

She had submitted her proposal for expanding her employer's business into France. If it was accepted, this would be her chance of promotion and a sojourn in Paris to set up the new company. Mike had been encouraging. He had come over and stayed last night, being especially tender and loving as if he wanted to make up for his recent non-appearance.

'Go for it,' he had said. 'I'd like nothing better than weekends with you in Paris, sitting out on the Champs Elysees, drinking wine into the small hours.'

'More likely watching rugby on the television,' she had retorted. Although she had laughed it off, in her mind's eye she saw them in a little apartment overlooking the Seine, having fresh crusty bread rolls and coffee for breakfast. Romantic evenings sitting out on one of those wrought-iron balconies which were so typical of Paris. A far cry from her little cottage here. She would probably see more of Mike than she did now, as he would have to make a special effort to fly over instead of simply getting in his car and dropping in on her at any time. Despite some doubts, the more she thought of it, the more enthusiastic she became at the prospect.

Piers looked up from his desk as she tapped on his door and entered his office. He was wearing his most serious expression.

'Sit down, Sherry. We need to talk.'

She took the chair on the other side of the desk and waited, feeling suddenly anxious. She recognized the file on his desk as her submission for the business expansion project. Vicky had put her report in early whereas she was a day late in submitting hers. Did that make him decide to disregard her submission? Or had he found some glaring error, some illogical conclusion to her take on how the opening of a new office in Paris should be handled? It was something that the company had never done before. Her mind ran over the main points she had raised. She had tried to view it from all angles and make a comprehensive list of the essential points. They seemed logical to her but might be very lacking in foresight from his point of view.

Piers looked down at the report on his desk and seemed to be reading it again, or at least part of it. Sherry waited, feeling the palms of her hands getting sticky with sweat.

Finally, Piers looked up at her. 'I think you need to do some more work on this,' he said in that serious tone he used on what he considered to be important business matters. 'I've marked off a few things which need more elucidation. I'd like you to get that done today as I have a board meeting first thing tomorrow morning and I'd like to present it to the board of directors for their consideration.'

Sherry left Piers' office with her head spinning. She had expected criticism, but this sounded as if he was pleased with what she had written. He had almost confirmed that she would be chosen to open the new office in Paris. Was this what in her heart of hearts she really wanted? She was going to have to make a decision soon.

CHAPTER FORTY-FOUR

Jessica rolled over in bed and checked the time on her mobile phone where it lay on the nightstand. It was only seven thirty but she knew she would not get back to sleep. Today was the day she was dreading, the day she was to appear in court, the date having been brought forward for some unknown reason. She had not told anybody about it, not even Ross when they had had their late lunch together a few days ago.

Thoughts of Ross made her smile despite the butterflies in her stomach and despite the dull headache which was the result of too much gin last night. They had spent a very enjoyable day together, late lunch had extended to a drive and then dinner at a small, intimate restaurant with dim lighting and soft background music. Ross seemed to know all the quaint little restaurants in a fifty-mile radius. The place was popular and Ross had had to exert his charm to get them a table. She was acutely aware that most of the diners were couples out for a romantic evening.

It was late when he had stopped outside her cottage. He turned to look at her in the darkness of the car.

'Want me to come in?'

Jessica found that her heart was starting to beat very fast. Part of her did not want the evening to end. It was up to her to invite him in, if that was what she wanted. He would not push her, she knew. Here was the choice she did not want to have to make.

'It's late. I'm sorry,' she found herself saying. 'Good night, Ross, and thanks for a lovely day.' She leaned over and kissed his cheek then exited the car quickly.

He waited until she had turned the key and let herself in, then with a wave of his hand he had driven away. She closed the door behind her and leant against it, trying to get her feelings under control. No, no, no, she told herself. You are not falling for him. You love Owen. And then the realization hit her that she had had far too much to drink tonight. If Ross had kissed her, who knows where it would have ended? I have to stop before I make a terrible mistake, she told herself, again.

When Jessica entered the courtroom, she was relieved that none of the faces were familiar to her. At least she was spared that humiliation. The hearing was brief and to the point. With no previous convictions, the judge treated her kindly. Three months driving ban with two months suspended and a modest fine to be paid to a charity of her choice. She breathed a sigh of relief as she walked out of the court building. She made a promise to herself to turn her life around and never again take a drop of alcohol if she were driving.

CHAPTER FORTY-FIVE

Millie signed the delivery driver's docket for the consignment of groceries and managed a cheerful smile at him. She was finding it hard to hold back the tears. Last night when she was putting the children to bed and Danny was brushing his teeth in the bathroom, Maeve had whispered to her. 'Danny's been stealing.'

Millie looked at the little girl's solemn expression – half important, half frightened - and had drawn her into her arms. 'Danny was stealing?'

'Yes, he was caught yesterday. He took Adam's money. Mrs Taylor's talked to him. Danny was crying.'

Millie's head reeled. Of all the things her children could be accused of, stealing was not one of them, she felt. She remembered that she had scolded them for playing in the yard of Fernwood House and Danny had been very upset about that. 'But Jason is so nice to us,' he had wailed. 'He told us we could play there any time.'

'I don't want you playing there and that's the end of it,' she had said, angry that they were apparently friendly with the very man who was planning to turn them out of their home.

Had this some negative effect on her son? Had he been looking for a replacement father? They never asked about their real father. She had told them that Kevin had emigrated and as far as she could tell, they had been satisfied with that. There would be questions when they got older, she knew, but for now they seemed happy enough.

She hugged Maeve now. 'Don't you worry. We'll get it sorted out,' she said, sounding far more confident than she felt. She had resolved to speak to Mrs Taylor before she broached the subject with Danny. It was probably a misunderstanding.

However, this morning Mrs Taylor had phoned her asking if she could come in after school today. Millie had agreed and now she was faced with the dilemma of getting someone to mind the shop in her absence because there was a scheduled delivery of goods due around that time. She had been depending on Mad Bobby and Jimbo but neither of them were contactable so far this morning. Mrs Donovan and her husband Podge were not available, as she knew. When Mrs Donovan collected the children for school this morning she had told Millie that she and her husband Podge both had hospital appointments.

An added problem which was occupying her this morning was that the children would be on their Halloween break from school next week and Mrs Donovan had hinted that she might not be available for a few days.

'Me daughter invited us to go away with them for the long weekend,' she said, not meeting Millie's eye. 'Sure you can have them in the shop with you for the few days.'

Millie knew this was true. Maeve and Danny could play upstairs in Mrs Foley's living room, could watch a bit of children's television and work on their painting books. She could probably leave them at home on the evenings when she did the cleaning for Alicia Scott-Douglas. It should not be a problem but with all the other things going on, it loomed large on her worries list.

The school was having two days of fun and games called Halloween Camp but this year Millie could not afford to send the children. Finances were stretched tight, especially as both children needed new winter shoes and there was the constant worry of having to find somewhere new to live.

Millie's thoughts buzzed around in her head like angry bees as she stacked the delivery goods. This needed to be done before the next consignment arrived later on today. Zac would normally be here to help with this but he was working on a garden project somewhere in the city and had to cancel his stint at Mrs Foley's shop. Had Danny really stolen a child's money? What would Mrs Taylor have to say? Was there anyone she could ask to look after the shop in her absence? She might have asked Lady Moll but knew that she was away visiting her sister. The delivery driver could put the goods round the back, of course, but she did not know him and feared he would be reluctant to do that. He probably needed a signature on the delivery docket. Tears of worry, of helplessness trickled down her cheeks as she worked.

The tinkle of the bell over the shop door alerted her to the arrival of a customer and she emerged from the storeroom at the back of the shop in time to see Jason DeVries walk in.

He gave her one of his rare smiles. 'Hi.' He waved what looked like a shopping list. 'I've run out of nearly everything, I think, so I'll just have a prowl around to see what I need to stock up on.'

Millie used her sleeve to brush the tears out of her face. He was the last person she needed to see right now. 'Let me know if I can help,' she said, not meaning a word of it.

He made no move to start shopping, instead he looked at her sharply. 'Something's wrong? Can I do something for you?'

There was genuine feeling in his voice and Millie was at her most vulnerable, which was the only explanation she could later give herself for breaking down, putting her face in her hands and bawling like a two-year old. Out it all came, the jumble of worries, Danny, the school, the shop, her words tripping over themselves. She did not make a lot of sense even to her own ears. The next moment, Jason had come and put his arm around her shoulders and given her a quick hug before hastily withdrawing. He stepped away from her without saying a word, simply waited for her crying to subside.

'Sorry.' Her voice was still muffled by the tears. 'Sorry. Sorry. I didn't mean to do that.'

There was a short pause before he spoke. 'Did I understand you need someone to mind the shop today?'

'I have to see Danny's teacher,' she said, 'and there's a consignment of bread and pastries due in. Zac would normally be here, but he's landed this gardening job and he needs the money. It's just for a few days and then he can take over again. I suppose I could leave a note for the driver and tell him to put everything round the back. Don't worry, it's my problem.'

'I'll do the shop,' he said in that firm no-arguments tone he had used to her before. 'Just show me what needs doing. I should be able to manage signing for a delivery. I promise not to eat any of the cakes. And if it comes to it, I'm sure I can handle the sale of a few litres of milk and a few pounds of butter, too.'

How she hated herself for bawling her eyes out in front of him. He was being nice and besides she had no alternative but to accept his help.

'That's very kind -,' she started to say but he cut her off.

'I'll drop you down to the school and then come back here to the shop,' he said. 'If you text me when you're finished, I'll pick you and the children up again after your meeting.'

Millie found herself meekly agreeing to let him know when to collect her that afternoon. Her uppermost feeling was relief that at least some of the problems of this morning were solved. The main surprise was that it was Jason DeVries, villain of the piece, who was helping her.

CHAPTER FORTY-SIX

'And you really think you have a good chance of being selected to set up the office in Paris?' Sherry's friend Bettina asked. Bettina, Lara and Liz were her closest friends. She had not met up with them in a long while mainly because of her other commitments. However, Bettina had today off and they had all agreed to meet for a few hours after work.

'I believe Piers presented my proposal to the board of directors this morning,' Sherry told her, eyes sparkling with excitement. 'Just imagine, living the life in gay Paree!'

Bettina laughed, then sobered again. 'It's a big step. What does Mike have to say about it?'

Bettina was the down-to-earth member of the little group. Lara and Liz had both been enthusiastic when she had told them about it. Lara had listed all the positives: promotion, more money, living in Paris, career chances. Bettina's was the only slightly critical voice.

'Mike thinks it's a great idea,' Sherry said quickly. She could not be cross with Bettina for voicing doubts but was anxious to dispel them. 'He says he'll be over to see me nearly every weekend.'

'Hmm.' Bettina stirred her half-finished cup of cappuccino, not looking directly at Sherry. 'Do you really think he will, though? He doesn't come round to your place half as often as he could. You're not hundreds of miles away after all, are you? I mean, he'll have to book a flight or flights to get to Paris. And he won't want to miss his rugby matches.'

Sherry thought she detected a slight frown from Liz directed at Bettina.

'He'll miss you far more than you or he thinks,' Lara put in quickly. Clearly she and Liz did not want to dampen Sherry's enthusiasm.

'I'm hoping that he'll miss me when I'm not in easy reach,' Sherry said. 'If we don't see each other for a few days now, he knows that he can come over and stay any time so it's no big deal. When he has to plan a bit and book flights, I'm sure it will be another story.' She forced a bright smile to hide the misgivings which she was already starting to feel. 'I know he won't be over every weekend. but I'll have things going on as well. It might be the best thing to happen to us.'

Bettina pursed her lips. 'Have you thought that you might get lonely? I mean, here at Fernwood Cottages you know everybody and everybody knows you. A long weekend in a strange city can be daunting. I know. I remember how I felt when I spent a month in New York, which is supposed to be one of the most exciting places in the world.'

'I plan on getting in a lot of sightseeing and I'm sure there'll be an Irish pub where I can meet up with other ex-pats. Anyhow, let's wait and see what Piers has to say.'

Bettina nodded. 'Yes, that makes sense, of course. But what about your project to stop the evictions at Fernwood Cottages? And the dog and cat rescue people depend on you, as well.'

Sherry gave a gusty sigh. 'I know. And you're right. I feel as if I'm letting everybody down if I take off for Paris. Then again, I keep telling myself it's the chance of a lifetime. They'll manage without me. No one is indispensable after all.'

'Are you making any progress on getting media attention about Fernwood?' Liz asked.

'I've been interviewed by local radio and two local newspapers have written up a piece on it.' She turned troubled eyes on her friends. 'I'm not confident that anything can be done. Millie and I spoke to Jason DeVries but I don't think we did any good. I'd hoped he might soften a bit when he knew about Millie being a single mother.' She threw up her hands in a gesture of despair. 'And the solicitor I consulted seemed to think that we didn't really have any legal wiggle room.'

'You've done your best. You'll make the right decision about Paris when the time comes.' Liz tried to console her.

'Let's see what happens,' Sherry said, trying her best to sound upbeat. 'Look, let's talk about something else. What have you three been doing with yourselves since I saw you last?'

Although the evening had produced a lot of light-hearted chatter, Bettina's words stayed with Sherry as she drove home that evening. Her first feelings of excitement were evaporating. She knew she would feel that she had abandoned the Fernwood Cottages residents if she left for Paris before she had explored every possible avenue to avert the loss of their homes. If only she could be sure that Mike really would come over at least every second weekend to visit her in Paris, a decision would be easier to make.

CHAPTER FORTY-SEVEN

Jessica was surprised to see Jason DeVries behind the counter of Mrs Foley's little shop when she popped in to get supplies. Before the incident with the car, she had rarely come to the shop. Now, however, she found it convenient. Living alone, her wants were few. She existed mainly on omelets, pasta and rice dishes, using meat from the freezer of which she still had a good supply. Today, however, she needed milk and bread.

She had not spoken more than two words to Jason, she reflected as she selected a small sliced pan from the shelf. He was probably the most disliked man in the neighbourhood, if Mrs Donovan was to be believed.

'If he was drowning, we wouldn't throw him a rope,' she had recently remarked when the subject came up. 'I hear he's moved into the big house. I suppose he wants to lord it over us before he sells us off.'

Jessica did not really know what to think about the situation. He was not her landlord, the cottage belonged to Owen. So far they had not heard from Jason DeVries and despite her suggestions that they approach him with a view to selling him the cottage, Owen was insistent that they wait until he was back home again and could pursue the matter directly himself.

'It's been in the family for ages,' he protested. 'I spent so many happy times there with nan and granddad. That's something I can't say about any other place I've lived in.'

'But that's only because your parents moved a few times,' Jessica had argued. 'The cottage was just a novelty and I'm sure your grandparents spoiled you and your brother and sisters rotten.'

Nevertheless, Jessica was curious how things were progressing with the sale of Fernwood Cottages.

'Has Mrs Foley given up the shop?' she asked with her most engaging smile as she put the litre of milk and the loaf of bread down on the counter to be checked out.

Jason looked a bit surprised at the question. 'No. At present nothing has changed.'

'Sorry. It's just that seeing you here behind the counter made me think that she had perhaps sold the place already.'

'You know she's in hospital?'

'Well yes, of course, but that would be a good reason to retire, I should have thought.' God, what do I sound like? She felt suddenly annoyed at herself. 'We'll all miss her. The shop is very convenient.' Now she was babbling to hide her embarrassment.

'I'm just filling in for Millie,' he said quietly as he started to ring up her purchases. 'I think this little neighbourhood is something else, the way they all help each other. I've never encountered anything like it until now.'

Jessica fished her bank card out of her purse and tapped in the payment. She did not have a word to say in reply. She stowed her purchases away and left the shop with his words ringing in her ears. Was she being totally unfair to her neighbours at Fernwood Cottages? Zac had helped her out with the car after the accident. When she had – finally - confessed to him that she would most likely lose her driver's licence, he had promised that he and Sherry would collect the vehicle as soon as the repairs were done. Considering that he hardly knew her, it was more, far more than she had expected. Millie had offered to help if needed and Lady Moll had made her a cake. Even nosy Mrs Donovan had offered to do her shopping for her and for the first few days after her accident had appeared at her door with a beef casserole and a shepherd's pie. 'You probably won't feel like cooking, love.'

Jessica knew that it was her frosty reception that had stopped Mrs Donovan and the others from offers of help after a few days. Was she being too hard on these people? For the first time since she had come here, she began to seriously question her attitude towards her neighbours at Fernwood Cottages and to ask herself if she should contribute something to help them in some way.

CHAPTER FORTY-EIGHT

Jason collected Millie punctually for her appointment with the school. They did not say much to each other on the drive. Her head was too full of worries about Danny's behaviour and Jason appeared preoccupied.

'Let me know when you're finished and I'll drop you home,' he said as she got out of his car. 'Good luck,' he added before she walked away.

Millie was shown into a little office next to the head teacher's quarters where Mrs Taylor awaited her.

'Are you having problems at home?' Mrs Taylor asked in a gentle tone when she had filled Millie in on what had been happening with Danny stealing from the other children. 'He's so good in school,' she had said. 'A bit mischievous like all little boys, but never any problem with his behaviour - until now that is.'

Millie was trying hard to suppress the tears that had started to well up. What could she say? There had been problems aplenty at home when she left Kevin and moved here to Fernwood Cottages. If Danny had been more difficult than normal during that awful time, she was not aware of it.

'We don't have problems at home,' she said slowly. 'I've no idea why Danny is doing this. It's just not like him.'

'Sometimes children play up in order to get attention, especially if they feel that something is going on which they can't understand.' Mrs Taylor gave her a shrewd glance before continuing. 'Children often play up if a parent has a new partner. They feel left out.' She let the sentence hang in the air.

Millie knew that Mrs Taylor had seen her get out of Jason's car. She probably assumed that they were a couple. In view of the animosity she felt towards Jason, the teacher could not have been wider of the mark.

'If you mean do I have a new partner, the answer is no, most certainly not,' she said firmly. 'I haven't spoken to Danny yet because I wanted to hear what you have to say first.' She thought for a minute or two. 'I'm very busy at the moment, running Mrs Foley's shop and then there's the few cleaning jobs I do. I suppose I don't have as much time for the children as I normally would.'

Her voice trailed away. She remembered the other night when the twins wanted her to read a second bedtime story and she had been cross with them for asking. Come to think of it, she was often cross with them these days if she were honest. But would that be the reason that Danny was stealing from his classmates? As far as she was aware Maeve was not affected in the same way or was it simply that she did not show how she felt? Was she being a bad mother, ignoring her children's needs?

Jason was waiting in his car for her when she left the school building with Danny and Maeve in tow. He got out and opened the car doors for them.

'How was school?' he wanted to know as they settled in the rear seats.

'Okay,' Danny said. He had a mulish expression on his face. 'We had a spelling game and I won,' Maeve told him.

'Good work.' Jason smiled at them and then slipped behind the wheel. He cast a glance at Millie. 'Jimbo and Mad Bobby have shown up to hold the fort at the shop. If your mum agrees we can go and have an ice-cream before I drop you home.'

'There's no need to bother,' Millie began but she was drowned out by both children squealing 'Ice-cream!'

Jason's mouth twitched. 'I think you've lost that argument.'

He drove them to the Italian café in Greenfields shopping centre and watched in amusement as the children pored over the menu.

Did he know just how rare such trips were for Maeve and Danny? Millie wondered as the waiter went off with their order. Money was always too tight for frequent treats. She settled for a latte while Jason chose a banana split for himself, much to her surprise. She would have thought that was too childish a choice for someone like him. It made him almost seem human. He surprised her still more by chatting to the children about their pastimes, what programmes they liked to watch on television, what stories they liked to read or have read to them. He seemed to be on the best of terms with the children. She remembered that he had told her that they played up in the yard at Fernwood House. Danny had been upset when she had forbidden them to go there again. Was that causing problems now? Surely not. She pushed the idea away.

She sat sipping her latte and watched Jason out of the corner of her eye as he listened to Maeve and Danny prattling on about school and play. Was this the monster who was turfing them out of their home? He probably felt guilty, she decided, but it would take a lot more than a few ice-cream sundaes to make up for the upset and worry he was causing.

Danny and Maeve managed to get ice-cream all over their faces and hands and went off to the rest room to clean up. When they had left the table, Jason turned to Millie. 'I have an idea. You mentioned that Mrs Donovan might not be able to take care of the children for a bit and I'd like to help you. I can drive them to and from school whenever you need, not a bad idea in this weather, and I can take over the afternoon shift in the shop. What do you say?'

She gaped at him. 'Take over the afternoon shift?'

He smiled. 'That's what I said and I meant it. Look, I don't want to know what that teacher had to say to you today, but I do know you can't do it all on your own. They're great kids, maybe they just need a bit more of your time. Think about it.'

Millie was at a loss as to what to say. Her feelings towards Jason and any help he offered were in turmoil. She had every reason to hate the sight of him, yet he had been kind to her several times, if she were honest.

'Why? Why are you doing this?' The words spilled out before she could stop them. 'We'll be gone in a few months and you'll have your fancy cottages to yourself. Why bother with us?'

He looked her straight in the eyes and the expression she saw there made her heart start to beat somewhere up in her throat.

'I'd like to tell you why,' he said softly. But before he could go on, Maeve and Danny arrived back at the table.

'Danny didn't dry his hands properly, they're all wet and he wet my blouse,' Maeve complained in a shrill little voice.

'No fighting, kids.' Millie spoke in her no-nonsense voice but it was as if a robot mouthed the words. She was still dazed over the turn her conversation with Jason had taken. She needed time to herself to get her head round it and try to understand where he was coming from. What would he have said to her? And why did some part of her, deep down, regret that the children had interrupted him?

CHAPTER FORTY-NINE

Sherry was a little surprised that she did not hear back from Piers on the Board's reaction to her proposal for setting up an office in Paris. He had made it seem fairly urgent. But perhaps he just wanted to show that he and his staff were on the ball. Piers was never backward in promoting his self-image to the higher powers. She debated asking Vicky if she had heard anything but decided against it. If Vicky had heard, she would gloat and if she did not, she would be immediately jealous that Piers had spoken to Sherry about her proposal.

There were other things on Sherry's mind today in any case. She had been working on her ideas for giving Mrs Foley's shop a much-needed facelift and had come up with a plan which needed Mrs Foley's approval. The Laurels, the nursing home where Mrs Foley was recuperating, was some distance away which necessitated Sherry leaving work early. She knew that the old lady was doing well – Millie kept in touch with her regularly by phone and kept all the neighbours up to date – and had no doubts that she would be able to listen and approve the plans Sherry had made.

In addition to her plans for improving the shop, Sherry was active in gathering information on tenancies and eviction of tenants and in finding affordable legal aid. Despite the excitement at the thought of moving to Paris, she found that the problems facing the tenants at Fernwood Cottages occupied her a good deal. She was fond of all her neighbours, even nosy Mrs Donovan. She wanted very badly to find a solution to the situation they all found themselves in.

'I don't know what you're worried about,' Mike had said the other night when she started talking about her plans. 'If you get the job in Paris, you're going to move out anyway, aren't you? Why go to all the bother?'

Sherry had bristled at the idea that she could abandon the Fernwood Cottage tenants without regrets. Deep down, she was disappointed, hurt even, that Mike did not suggest that she could move in with him if they all had to leave their homes.

The Laurels was a big modern-built building surrounded by fields and woods. Sherry cast an appreciative eye over the grounds as she drove up the short avenue and parked at the rear of the building. Mrs Foley came to meet her, leaning heavily on a walking stick, and they sat down in one of the little rooms reserved for private visits. It was a pleasant room with a view of the well-tended garden. Brightly patterned curtains and a bowl of flowers on the table added to the feeling of good cheer. She was lucky to be able to afford this private nursing home, Sherry thought, and again the question raised itself about who was paying for it? Mrs Foley's sister could certainly not afford it. The subject occupied all the neighbours at Fernwood Cottages but no one had come up with a satisfactory explanation although Mrs Donovan sometimes surmised that either Mrs Foley or her sister had won on the national lottery and were keeping it quiet.

'I have some ideas about the shop,' Sherry said when they had exchanged the usual small talk. 'If you've no objection, I'd like to get a coffee machine and maybe organize a supply of sandwiches. It would make people stay longer in the shop and buy more stuff. Besides, if you think about it, the shop isn't too far from the main road and a lot of motorists drive that way when they're going to the coast. You could have outdoor seating in the summer, too.'

She looked anxiously at the frail old lady sitting in the armchair opposite her. They were all so used to Mrs Foley bustling about, full of energy, that it was a shock to see her like this.

Mrs Foley leant forward and patted Sherry's hands where they lay in her lap. 'You're very good, love. Thanks a million for all you've done.' She shook her head and gave the ghost of a smile. 'But I couldn't afford anything like that. And anyway as we're being evicted, it's hardly worth me while is it, to spend thousands of euros – pounds I was going to say – on doing the place up?'

Sherry had been prepared for this argument. 'It won't cost that much,' she said. 'We'll do a bit of fundraising. Zac has promised to help out any way he can, so we'll come up with some good ideas.'

'Zac would do anything for you, wouldn't he, love? I don't know why you don't let him marry you.'

'Zac? Marry Zac?' Sherry laughed but the colour burned in her cheeks. 'I doubt if he'd have me if I wanted to.'

Mrs Foley watched her out of wise old eyes. 'He's in love with you for years. You must know that. Sure, he'd be ideal for you.'

'Are you taking up match-making now?' Sherry tried to laugh it off. Mrs Foley seemed to have forgotten about Mike.

'I know what I see.' Mrs Foley's smile was enigmatic.

Sherry judged it time to move on with the conversation. 'Now, if we can raise enough money, you'll be OK with getting in the coffee machine and sandwiches? A lot of people ask, you know, so Millie tells me. Commuters like coffee to go and something to eat as well.'

'If you can come up with the money, by all means. But like I said, what's the point when whats-his-name is throwing us out?'

'We're going to fight that.' Sherry spoke with more confidence than she felt. 'I've found a solicitor who's prepared to help us.' She did not add that the said solicitor, Walter Dunne, was very dubious about the success of the venture.

'A solicitor? Sure they cost a fortune. He won't be doing it for nothing, I'm sure.'

'I've found a fellow that only gets paid if he's successful. Of course we'd have to pay reasonable expenses, but no win no fee is how he works.'

'And you believe that?'

Sherry was well aware that the "reasonable expenses" would most likely be anything but reasonable. The fighter in her refused to give in to negativity. She noticed now that Mrs Foley was getting tired, that these ideas were too much for her to take in, or at least any further discussion of them.

'I'll be back to see you to let you know how we're getting on,' she said, rising from her seat. 'Don't worry. Everything will work out. The most important thing is that you get back on your feet again. Everyone is asking how you're doing. We're lost without you around.'

The old lady smiled. 'That's a sweet thing to say.'

'It's true, though.' As she took leave of the old woman, Sherry had the satisfaction of seeing her expression brighten. Now all I've got to do is see this through, come hell or high water, she thought.

CHAPTER FIFTY

Jessica was more conscious stricken about her neglect of what was going on around her than she had been at any time since she moved here. Her conversation with Jason DeVries kept coming back to her. Should she do something to help Millie? But working in the shop was not her thing. She just would not have the patience to deal with these people. What else could she do? She decided at last that she would offer to look after Millie's two children while Millie was working in the shop. When she got her driving licence back, she could even drop them off at school and collect them again.

Yes, she decided, she would do something like that. It was being neighbourly.

Mindful of the fact that she and Owen would be away for a week around the second week of November at the latest as he had assured her, she decided to wait before speaking to Millie about her idea. Owen had still not given her a definite date and she was still deciding where she and Owen should go. When she knew what their plans were, she would volunteer her services.

Having settled these ideas with herself, she turned her attention to finding a romantic location for her week away with Owen. She was flicking through the travel pages of a woman's magazine and perusing the comments on various resorts over a mug of coffee – she had managed to stay off the gin so far today - when Ross came knocking at her door.

'Hi there,' he said. 'I've been thinking about you. Fancy a drive somewhere?'

He looked very handsome as he stood in the middle of her kitchen. Her heart gave a little flutter in spite of herself. His eye caught the magazine open on the table in front of her with pictures of the blue Mediterranean sea and glistening white-walled hotels complete with sun-worshippers lounging around swimming pools.

'Are you looking for a sunny getaway? Not that I blame you with this awful weather.'

They both looked instinctively out of the window at the rain which was sheeting down.

'Owen and I are planning a week away in November. He'll be finished his tour by then.'

'I see.' He pushed both hands into the pockets of his jeans and looked away from her. 'I can't pretend I'm not jealous.'

'Don't be silly.' It was all she could think of to say. She was pleased to see him but that wasn't a crime, she told herself. He was fun to be with but there was no way she would ever be unfaithful to Owen.

'I wish I was being silly.' He looked at her then and the expression in his eyes made the breath catch in her throat. 'My bad. Have pity on me and come for a drive? I need some sunshine in my life.'

She knew that she should be sensible, that she should stop this now before one of them got hurt, but the idea of being in his company was hard to resist. She really enjoyed being out with him, she had not had such fun in years. But that didn't make it right, she reminded herself.

'Don't you have to work at your salon today?'

'I've given myself time off for good behaviour.' He laughed. 'Come on. I need your advice. I've been looking for a house and I might have found just the right place. I've got the keys from the estate agent and I'd love to get your opinion on it. What do you say? I'll take you to dinner as a thank you.'

She was flattered that he wanted her opinion and the idea of going out with him on this dreary day was very appealing. Besides, giving her opinion on his house-hunting options was respectable, not really "going out" as such. 'All right, but I'm not an expert on housing.'

His face lit up. 'Good girl. Let's go.'

'I'll be right out, just need to get my coat.'

While he walked to his car, Jessica hastily rummaged in the cupboard for the bottle of gin and took a few hefty slugs of the liquid. She needed a drink to help her relax and be good company, she reasoned, pushing away her guilty feelings. As she shrugged into her coat, she cast a quick glance at the travel brochures on the table, lying there like a reproach. There would be time enough to choose a destination tomorrow when Owen would telephone her.

'I didn't know you were moving house,' she said as they drove away.

'I've been looking for a place for some time,' he told her. 'It's hard to find somewhere in the suburbs that's affordable. I don't want to live in isolated splendour in the country.'

They debated the various merits of living in the city with all the traffic but also all the conveniences as opposed to a country residence. Jessica was a city person, she had grown up in a large town and during her married life, owing to Owen's job, she had lived in New York, Brussels, Berlin and lastly in London. Cottage life was certainly not for her and Ross heartily agreed with her.

By the time they arrived at the house which Ross wanted to view, Jessica felt completely justified in her opposition to Owen's ideas of living in the cottage. Owen was being selfish. Ross, on the other hand, understood her sentiments completely.

The house Ross wanted to view was on a quiet tree-lined avenue. It had a good-sized front garden which was beginning to show signs of neglect. Ross produced the keys and ushered her into the spacious hall. Jessica fell in love with the place instantly. If only she was viewing it with Owen, she thought, as they ambled from room to room, she would have wanted to buy it straight away.

Ross was very thorough in his inspection of the place. The rear garden needed landscaping he said and the smaller living room – there were two – could be turned into an office. The kitchen was a bit small, it could do with the addition of a laundry room and a separate larder.

'I didn't know you were so domesticated,' Jessica had laughed. She wondered not for the first time if he had been married before.

They spent a long time going over the place. Despite enjoying Ross' company, Jessica began to feel the effects of those slugs of gin starting to wear off. She badly needed another drink and was relieved when Ross checked his watch.

'I don't know about you but I'm getting hungry,' he said, let's go and find somewhere to eat. We could try The Postillion, it's not too far away.' He certainly knew all the best places to eat.

'Do you think you'll buy the place?' she asked as they were sipping pre-dinner drinks in the stylish restaurant. The sting of the gin going down was making her feel better already.

'I'm not sure.' Ross thought for a bit. 'It's pricey. I'll have to talk to my bank manager.'

'It really is a lovely place and a very good location.' She finished her drink and looked around for the waiter to signal she wanted a refill. To her relief, Ross did not seem to mind or indeed notice how much she drank.

'I know who I'd like to share it with,' he said, raising his glass to her. 'You're a beautiful woman and so much fun to be around.'

'Thanks for the compliment.' Jessica managed to keep the tone light. They seemed to be within half a sentence of getting serious which she didn't want. Ross took the hint and the meal progressed very pleasantly. The wine flowed freely and she could relax. It was only when Ross pulled up outside her cottage that she felt unsure of herself again.

He switched off the engine and turned to look at her. 'Are you going to ask me in?'

'It's been a lovely day, Ross and thank you for that. But it's late and I really think –'

He cut her short. 'Jess, listen to me. I know that your husband will be home soon and we won't see each other again. I want to make love to you.'

For some reason tears formed in a lump at the back of her throat and she could not say a word.

'How do you feel about going away for a weekend with me?'

She swallowed hard, struggling to make light of the situation. They had both had a bit to drink, she reminded herself. 'I bet you say that to all the girls.'

He did not answer her smile. 'I don't. Believe me, I've never said it or wanted to say it to any woman until now. I've never met anyone like you, Jessica. I think you feel something for me, too. Be kind. We'll always have that memory. What have you got to lose?'

CHAPTER FIFTY-ONE

Jason was as good as his word and turned up at Millie's next morning to take the children to school. Maeve and Danny were delighted to be getting a lift, especially as there was a gusting wind that hurled the raindrops against the cottage windows.

Millie had not really expected him. She did not know how she felt about seeing him again, it would have been better if he had not come, she felt. For the children's sake, she kept her protests to herself.

Jason appeared in good spirits, teasing the children about school before ushering them into the back of his car and handing them in their school bags.

Before he got into the driving seat, he turned to Millie who was standing in the doorway watching.

'You look like you swallowed a tadpole,' he said in a low voice so that Maeve and Danny could not hear. 'Bear up. You'll get used to it. I'll collect the kids after school and I can take over at the shop for a few hours this evening.'

'All right,' she found herself saying. She had tossed and turned last night after that conversation with him at the ice cream parlour. What had he meant? What would he have said if they had not been interrupted? And what would or could she have said in return? She had found no answers to her dilemma as she waited for morning to come. Today she was too tired to think straight or to react to what was happening. Not that Jason seemed to need any discussion.

She watched the car drive off, the children chattering happily in the back seat, enjoying the novelty of being driven to school. At least they would be out of the rain, she told herself. Just then Mrs Donovan appeared, brandishing an umbrella. She turned and stared after Jason's car.

'Was that his lord and mighty? With the children?' She made it sound as if Jason was leading them to the guillotine.

Millie bit her lip. 'Oh Mrs Donovan, I'm so sorry I didn't get to tell you that Jason is going to drive the children to and from school for the present.'

Mrs Donovan screwed up her mouth in that way she had to show total disapproval. 'Jason, is it? You're getting very pally with him, aren't you? I hear he drove you to see Mrs Foley a couple of times.'

'We're not pally,' Millie said, 'he's just being helpful. He probably feels bad about throwing us all out of our homes.'

'Hmm.' Mrs Donovan scowled. 'So he should be. I hope you give him a good telling off. He doesn't care about anyone.'

Somewhere, deep down inside, Millie could not agree with Mrs Donovan. She felt that he did care about what happened to them all but was unwilling or unable to put it into words. He had seen that she needed help and had stepped in without making a fuss or wanting thanks. What was happening? Why did she no longer know where she stood in relation to her feelings for Jason DeVries? How could you even begin to like someone who was throwing you out of your home?

CHAPTER FIFTY-TWO

Sherry had only just arrived home from work when Zac popped his head round the door. 'Feel up to going for a drink? You've been working like a mad woman all week. Time to have a break.'

For the first time in their acquaintance, Sherry felt ill at ease in Zac's company. She had Mrs Foley to thank for that, she knew. 'He's in love with you for years,' she had said. If she were asked, Sherry would have said that she and Zac were close friends. They saw a lot of each other, always popping in and out of each other's houses, watching television shows together or simply having a chat and sharing local news. They were soul mates. But was she in love with him or he with her? She loved Mike, why would she even question her feelings for Zac?

'I've only just got in.' She shrugged off her coat and hung it up by the door.

If he noticed a certain coolness in her tone, he did not show it. 'I made shepherd's pie,' he said. 'Fancy some?'

She hesitated. If he really had feelings for her, it was up to her to slowly distance herself from their relationship. He knew that she was crazy about Mike, so he would know that he had no chance with her. How to be kind and not hurt his feelings?

'What's the matter?' He asked now, always alert to her moods.

'Nothing. I suppose I am tired.'

'You'll feel better when you've eaten something.'

He had already set the table, she found when they went to his cottage. 'Glass of wine?' he asked as he served them generous portions of the shepherd's pie.

'No thanks, I'll fall asleep if I drink anything alcoholic.' This was only partly true but she wanted to be clear-headed. Was this the end of the relaxed, confidential discussions about anything and everything which they so often had? She would be very sorry to miss those late-night conversations over a glass of Beaujolais, her favourite tipple, to no longer have someone with whom she could feel totally at ease.

She found herself looking at Zac as if he were a new acquaintance. He was attractive although not goodlooking in the conventional sense, rugged would best describe him. He was dressed as usual in shabby jeans and a many-times-washed sweatshirt. There was something about him, some quality which she found hard to name, which usually made her feel better just at the sight of him. Tonight was different but that was her own fault, as she was only too aware.

He had been out most of the day working on an overgrown garden in a housing estate, he told her. 'What about you, Sher? Have you heard from Piers about your proposal?'

'I haven't seen Piers today,' she confessed. 'I've been tied up with this new client of ours who wants me to produce a miracle marketing plan in two days. And I've been looking at coffee making machines for Mrs Foley's shop. I've seen one that I'm going to get out of my own money and she can pay me back whenever it's convenient. I have to wonder, though, if we're all not wasting our time when we've only got six months to find somewhere else to live or to fight the eviction.'

'Have you spoken to Jason DeVries?'

She shook her head. 'Not since Millie and I met with him. I told you about that. I can't see him changing his mind. I thought Millie's situation, with the children and all that, would make him think it over.'

'You've done your best. Look, just switch off tonight. If you don't want to go out for a drink, just sit around listening to music, clear your head. Have an early night.' He grinned at her. 'I know. I sound like your mother.'

'There's one thing,' she said slowly, 'I thought today that if Piers came on bended knee and offered me that job in Paris, that somehow or other I'd say no and be done with it.'

Zac looked at her quickly. 'I don't think you mean that, do you? You told me you'd like nothing better than the challenge. Are you afraid that there'll be trouble with Mike if you really were to take off for foreign soil?'

She buried her face in her hands. 'I don't know what to think, to be honest. I know I'd miss Fernwood Cottages, yes even nosy Mrs Donovan.' And you, Zac, she thought but did not say aloud.

He came and put an arm around her shoulders in a quick hug before moving away from her again.

'I'm here, any time you want to talk.'

Yes, she thought, you're always there for me, Zac. That's partly the problem. I hate the thought that a move to Paris would mean not having you living next door to me, you not there to cheer me up on days like today. That doesn't mean that I don't love Mike, he's all the world to me.

CHAPTER FIFTY-THREE

Jessica was relieved when Zac and Sherry collected her car from the repair shop, although the size of the bill made her wince. She would have to tell Owen what had happened since he would see the transaction on the online bank statement. He would be mad at her. And he would most likely want to know if she had been drinking. Just once, many years ago, she had driven home from a party while she was a bit tipsy. Owen had been very angry. 'Just suppose you killed someone because your reactions at the wheel weren't what they should be' he had stormed. Alcohol had never played a big part in her life until now. But since she had moved to Fernwood Cottages, her intake had increased considerably. She knew this was from loneliness, knew that she should find something to occupy herself but that one disastrous interview for the job at The Snow Queen had made her reluctant to try again.

After poring over various holiday destinations, she finally decided on a luxury hotel near Lu Impostu beach in Sardinia. As she studied the pictures, she could almost feel the warm sun on her body, could visualize lazy days on the beach, outdoor dinners and romantic nights with Owen, their bedroom windows thrown open to the balmy night air and the gentle sound of the surf breaking on the beach. It really would be a second honeymoon.

She made a note of the costs, ready for when Owen would ring her. Once she had made the reservations, she would really start looking for a job of some kind and she would also offer to help Millie with the children, she promised herself. And most important of all, she would cut down drastically on her drinking. Her ankle was much improved so that she could return to the fitness studio at Greenfields.

Owen rang her earlier than she had expected. She was just about to prepare a toasted cheese sandwich for lunch.

'What happened to the car?' He wanted to know after the briefest of greetings. 'I see that you made a big payment to Whiddy's Garage.'

'I had a bit of an accident. It's all fixed now, so no harm done. Listen, I've found the perfect place for our few days away –'

'What do you mean "a bit of an accident"? What happened? Were you hurt?'

'I got dazzled by another car's lights and had to brake. I got into a spin and hit a concrete pillar. There was a bit of damage to a wall, too, and we'll be getting a bill for the repairs to that. It shouldn't be too high. I'm fine, just a few bruises and a twisted ankle but that's much better now. Zac, one of the neighbours came on the scene and got the car towed to Whiddy's. I'd have been lost without him.'

If she was hoping that he would show her some sympathy, she was mistaken as his next question showed. 'Were you drinking, Jess?'

'I'd had a drink or two but I wasn't drunk if that's what you mean.'

'That **is** what I mean. Just how many drinks did you have that night?'

He sounded angry, very angry, and she couldn't really blame him.

'A few,' she said. 'I'm sorry, I really am. It's never going to happen again, I promise.'

'The gardai were involved, I take it?'

'Yes.'

'Come on Jess, what are you hiding? You'd have told me long ago unless something wasn't right. Were you breathalysed? Did you lose your licence?'

How well he knew her, she thought.

'I got a suspended sentence, a three months ban with two months suspended because I've no previous record and anyway, the judge was very nice about it. I've really learned my lesson.'

There was silence on the other end of the line for a full two minutes. She could hear his breathing, so knew he had not hung up. 'Jess,' he said slowly, have you been drinking and driving before this happened? Were you out on your own? That's different from having a few drinks with friends, that can happen, even if it shouldn't. Maybe you should have a think about where you're going. Talk to someone about it.'

'What do you mean?' She felt as if he had slapped her.

'I mean that you shouldn't have driven the car if you'd had a few drinks. You know how strict the law is, quite apart from the danger of injuring somebody. Was anyone injured?'

'No. I told you. I hit a concrete pillar.'

'Where were you coming from?'

'I was in town and had dinner there.'

'Were you out with Zac?'

The chill in his voice caused her to start in surprise.

'Out with Zac? Of course not.'

Again that long pause before he spoke. 'All right. But get some counselling sorted for yourself, Jess. It's important.'

'I will, I promise.' She hesitated before asking 'Don't you want to hear about the place I've found for our little getaway?'

'Not now, Jess. I haven't time. I've got to go. Talk soon.'
He rang off without the usual "love you, Jess."

CHAPTER FIFTY-FOUR

With Halloween approaching and the Donovans visiting family down the country, Jason DeVries drove Millie's children to school and took over the shop from her for the last two hours in the evenings. He did not try to have a private conversation with her again. It was an awkward situation and she had no other option but to accept it. Danny and Maeve were delighted with him, chattering about what he had said today. He made them laugh a lot which was hard for her to accept. Something had to give, she knew, but for now she tried to shut her eyes to the situation.

The coffee machine was duly installed. Lady Moll volunteered to make scones and sandwiches every day and to Millie's surprise, more customers than usual came to the shop. Jimbo and Mad Bobby also did their share of serving in the shop. This ensured that Millie had more time with the children while still working two of her regular cleaning jobs and she had even been able to take on a third one. The children seemed happy which gave her reason to hope that Danny would not cause any more trouble in the future.

Despite Sherry's optimism that their eviction would be halted, Millie began searching for affordable accommodation for them. She was now on the waiting list for social housing. 'There is a long waiting list, I'm afraid,' the woman in the housing office told her. 'You might have to stay in a hotel sharing with other families, at least in the short term.'

Millie felt sick at the thought. She loved the freedom of living in Fernwood Cottages with the open countryside on her doorstep.

Jason surprised her one evening a few days before the Halloween school break when he came to take over the shop. 'If you still want to use that corner of the grounds by the stream, you can,' he said, sounding a bit offhand as she handed him the shop keys. 'Danny and Maeve were saying how much they liked playing there. So feel free.'

'Thank you.'

He really was nice and so good with the children and if she let herself, she could like him, more than like him. Here she pulled herself up short. When she left Kevin, she had resolved never to let a man get too close to her ever again. There had been that single father at the PTA meeting last year who had asked her out. He was pleasant and quite goodlooking, but she had felt completely spooked and had said no. Recently, when she noticed the way Jason looked at her, she felt spooked again. I'm better off on my own, she told herself, and besides I can't do this to Maeve and Danny.

'Another thing,' Jason said as she turned to go. 'The children were talking about the circus that's coming to town on Saturday. They'd love to go to it. Could you – would you – I mean, I'd like to invite you and the children if that's all right?'

It was the first time that he sounded unsure of himself. This was so completely out of character that it threw Millie off balance. Jason DeVries had always sounded as if he had no doubts about himself and what he wanted. She did not know what to make of this new version of him.

She stared at him for a moment. 'I couldn't possibly expect you to do that. But thank you,' she added lamely. What had he said to her the other day? 'You look like you swallowed a tadpole?' She probably looked like that now, too.

'The children would love it. I thought we could take them to McDonalds afterwards. If you're worried about the shop, I spoke to Jimbo and Mad Bobby today and they would be more than happy to fill in on Saturday.'

While she was still searching for a reply, he went on. 'The kids were talking about it today. They'd love to go. I'd enjoy it myself and I think you could do with some time out. Come on, don't be stubborn. I won't eat you.'

Millie knew about the circus and had been debating taking the children to see the performance. It would be the only outing that she could afford, and she was not even sure that she could afford that. Was she being stupidly stubborn? She could imagine how ecstatic Maeve and Danny would be at the prospect of an afternoon at the circus with a visit to McDonalds afterwards for good measure. There were not too many really exciting events in their lives.

'All right,' she found herself saying. 'It's very good of you. The children will be so pleased.'

She wanted to ask him why he was doing this but remembering his remark in the ice cream parlour when she had asked him that question, she didn't have the courage. A small voice, which she was trying hard to bury, asked her if she was afraid of what Jason would say and even more afraid of what her reaction would be. He could be as nice and helpful as he liked, she reasoned with herself, but the fact remained that he was throwing her and the children and nearly all of the residents at Fernwood Cottages out of their homes. Why couldn't he just continue being as curt and unpleasant as he had at the beginning of their acquaintance?

He smiled at her now. 'Wonderful. The performance starts at three o'clock. I'll pick you and the children up at half past two on Saturday, if that's all right?'

'That's fine. We'll be ready. Thank you.' She shrugged into her coat already looking forward to the children's reaction when she told them.

'I have to thank you,' he said and there was an undercurrent to his tone which made her heart race.

Millie paused with her hand on the doorknob. Maybe it was time to clear the air so that he did not have any unreasonable expectations.

'I'm very grateful for – for the children's sake,' she said, not meeting his gaze.

Without waiting for his reaction, she hurried out into the cold night air.

CHAPTER FIFTY-FIVE

Sherry was very pleased with the prompt delivery of the coffee machine and also with Lady Moll's offer of making scones and sandwiches. Lady Moll would bake for any and every occasion. The residents of Fernwood Cottages were a little in awe of her because of her love of literary quotes and what they considered to be high-brow interests. She played Bridge every Sunday night at the community centre in Greenfields and always baked a cake or two to accompany the tea and coffee afterwards. If there were any leftovers, she divided these between Mad Bobby and Jimbo despite disapproving of their drinking.

Sherry learned from Millie that the number of customers coming to the shop had increased, something which she put down to her own marketing skills and to Lady Moll's reputation as a maker of delicious cakes and scones. She had contacted the local radio station and also the local newspaper and had talked about Mrs Foley's shop and what it meant to the neighbourhood. As always, stories with human interest were popular and proving a good marketing ploy.

The news from Walter Dunne, the solicitor she had consulted, was not so rosy. 'I've written to the estate agents, since they were the ones issuing the termination of tenancy,' he explained. 'They'll pass on my letter to the new owners. It'll take time, mind you.'

Sherry felt that they did not have that much time. She was especially concerned about Mrs Foley and the shop. She had visited her again recently to confirm the purchase of the coffee machine and tell her of the improvement in the number of customers coming to the shop.

'Well done, love' Mrs Foley had said. 'Sure, the shop will be as big as Harrods of London by the time you've finished.'

'It won't do any harm to have a few more things in stock,' Sherry told her.

Mike had been less than enthusiastic when she spoke to him about her plans over dinner the previous night.

'Are you sure it's worth all the hassle? I mean, there's a very good chance that you'll be off to Paris after Christmas. And Mrs Foley will lose her tenancy, like everyone else.'

'It's not only about me. I'm doing this for the people here. They don't deserve to be thrown out just because someone buys Fernwood Estate.'

'The people here, as you call them, probably won't even thank you. And anyway, didn't you say you were going to approach DeVries about getting some kind of compensation for them?'

'Millie and I already spoke to him – I thought I'd mentioned it? He did say he would be prepared to help with finding accommodation but how he would do that is anyone's guess, if I'm honest. At the moment he is being very kind and is driving Millie's children to school and even doing a few hours in the shop. Hard to fathom what's going on in his mind. I don't want to rock the boat for Millie but we will have to talk to him again at some stage.'

Mike shook his head at her. 'Lady Moll would quote that thing about tilting at windmills – from Don Quixote, right?

Trying to fight the impossible or something. Why don't you just leave it and concentrate on your day job?'

Sherry was getting angrier by the minute. 'You mean, I'd see more of you if I just did my nine to five bit and waited in every evening?'

He waved his hands in the air. 'Don't go there, Sherry.'

'Why not? We don't get to see each other that much these days. Either you're playing rugby or training to play rugby or you have some event or other from work.'

'And what about you? If you're not dropping off dog food at The Haven, organizing concerts and fighting the good fight, you're too tired to be much company.' This was a dig at her because she had been yawning over the meal, she felt.

'I'm sorry I'm such boring company. Maybe you should try going out to dinner with someone else.'

'You know what, Sherry? That was just what I was thinking myself. Let's have a break from each other, OK? I think we need a cooling off period to know what we want.'

She stared at him. It took her a minute to find her voice. 'Do you really mean that?'

He began to pace up and down, his hands thrust into his pockets. 'Yes, I do think it would be a good idea to cool it for a while.'

Perhaps, deep down, she had seen this situation coming. Mike had always been less than supportive of the various activities she was involved in, more so of late. She had tried to laugh it off, to pretend she did not mind, that he was busy or a thousand other excuses for his behaviour. He had not come to her sister's engagement party and he was avoiding giving her an answer when she asked him what they were doing for Christmas. Her mother and indeed her sister were fully expecting to see them over the approaching holiday season. Was it the end of the road for their relationship? They had been together for such a long time. He had always been there in the background. It couldn't end like this. What would she do without him?

CHAPTER FIFTY-SIX

Jessica did not hear from Owen for a longer period than usual. He had mentioned that he had added a few more places to his itinerary but she had not paid much attention to the details. When he did ring, no mention was made of either the car repairs or her drinking. They spoke mainly about the children. The call was briefer than usual but, in a way, Jessica was glad of that. There would be enough opportunity for talking things over when they had their time away together. She gave him the details of the hotel in Sardinia and he sounded pleased, only requesting that she hold off on booking it until he had an exact date for his return flight.

Meantime she had enough things to occupy her thoughts. Did Owen really think she was having an affair with Zac? Was that because he himself had met someone? We have to trust each other she thought. If we can't do that, then we are lost.

Instinct told her that if Owen ever discovered that she had been going out with Ross on a regular basis, he would never believe that nothing had happened between them, no matter what she said. She had been very careful with Ross, never inviting him in after an evening out, especially when she'd had a few drinks. She had done nothing wrong, except perhaps keep it from Owen. The thought of giving up Ross' company was an unwelcome one, but she loved Owen and did not want to endanger her marriage.

The most pressing thing was to show Owen that she was looking for help with her drinking. She had occasionally had too much to drink at parties or at those formal dinners with Owen. But she had never had alcohol every day or even felt the need of it. What was becoming of her?

She started searching for information on counselling. The idea of simply going along to an Alcoholics Anonymous meeting did not appeal to her. She would try and find person-to-person treatment. I'm not really an alcoholic, she told herself as she scrolled down through the various websites on her laptop, I just need to cut down. Perhaps what she needed was to do some kind of further education course? A scroll through the internet revealed that the majority of courses started in September, too late to enrol now. Besides, she was not sure exactly what she wanted to study.

She was in the middle of researching information on private colleges in the area in the hopes of getting some idea of what she could do, when Ross tapped at her door and came in without waiting for an invitation. The front door of the cottages led straight into the kitchen. None of the tenants at Fernwood Cottages ever locked their doors during the day which meant casual visitors came straight in. Jessica had fallen into this habit of not locking her door, too. Ordinarily she would not have minded that he appeared in her kitchen, but she would have preferred if he did not see what she was researching on the internet.

'Hi there,' he said, coming up to where she was sitting and planting a kiss on the back of her head. 'You look like you're hard at work.'

As always, her heart gave a little teenager type flutter at the sight of him. She closed the programme, clicked the Exit button on the laptop and stood up. 'Just browsing,' she said lightly.

'What are you up to, Ross? Have they thrown you out at the salon?'

He laughed at that but then became serious almost immediately. 'I've come with a proposition. You told me Owen won't be home until the middle of the second week of November or thereabouts, so I thought we could have our time this coming weekend.' As she opened her mouth to object, he held up a hand. 'Wait a sec. Let me finish. I've been given the option of staying at a lovely little villa in the south of France. Sounds like a cliché, doesn't it? But actually, a friend of a friend owns it and he's willing to let us stay there for a few nights. It's near Cannes. Near the beach. It has a swimming pool and it's all private. What do you say?'

For a glorious moment her imagination conjured up a chateau, grey stone walls surrounding it, a garden terrace full of flowers and beyond that the deep blue of the sea reflecting the cloudless sky. And Ross. The thought brought her feet firmly back to earth with a thump. She took a few steps away from him.

'I'm not asking for us to have an affair,' he said, watching her face intently as if trying to read her emotions. 'I'm just asking for a few days, a few nights with you. Just the two of us. I really, really want to make love to you, Jess.'

'And you think we could come home and just forget it ever happened? I have a husband, Ross. I couldn't do that to him.'

'I'm not trying to take anything away from your husband. I want to give you something – to give you memories of our time together. Something neither of us will ever forget.'

'I can't. You know I can't.' She blinked away the sudden tears that formed at the back of her eyes. Why was she crying? For herself? For Ross?

'Jess, darling.' Ross crossed the room in two strides. He took her face in his hands and very gently wiped away the tear that had spilled over onto her cheek. Then he began to kiss her, wildly, passionately. Something stirred deep inside her and she found herself responding almost against her will.

CHAPTER FIFTY-SEVEN

Remembering her parting remark the other evening, Millie would not have been too surprised if Jason had backed out of the visit to the circus on Saturday, but promptly at two thirty his big BMW slid to a halt outside her cottage. Maeve and Danny were buzzing with excitement.

'There he is,' they screamed in unison, dashing out of the door and climbing into the back of the vehicle without waiting for her.

'Got everything?' Jason asked laconically as she took the passenger seat beside him.

She avoided looking at him. 'Yes, thank you.'

What would they talk about on the drive to the circus? she wondered. Jason was not good at small talk at the best of times as she knew only too well from their various drives together to see Mrs Foley. She need not have worried. Maeve and Danny kept up a barrage of questions, speculating about what was likely to be on the programme based on the posters advertising the circus which were on display all over the neighbourhood.

When they got to the field where the circus tent had been erected, both children espied some friends from school and raced off to talk to them.

'They're having fun,' Jason said with a laugh. 'Makes me almost wish I was eight years old again. Did you go to a circus when you were a kid?'

'Once or twice, yeah.' At least they were on safe ground with this subject. 'What about you?'

He launched into a story from his childhood about his grandmother taking him to see a circus and how terrified of the clowns he had been. They walked towards the circus tent as they spoke. Millie called the children who came rather reluctantly.

'Can I sit with Paul and Eoin?' Danny asked.

'And I want to sit with Tessa and Maria,' Maeve said.

Millie had not foreseen this and for a moment she was at a loss. Did she want to sit through the circus with only Jason DeVries for company? Most definitely not. She knew, however, that if she objected, both children would create a scene and even worse, they would want to know why in that way that children have of picking on things that can't be easily explained.

'All right,' she said, not looking at Jason to see how he took this arrangement. 'But remember to behave yourselves, no fighting with the other kids.'

'We won't,' they assured her.

'Let's get you all some popcorn first,' Jason said and shepherded the twins and their friends to the little counter at the back of the tent. Millie trailed in their wake, pleased to see Danny and Maeve so happy but not so pleased that Jason was the cause of it.

When the children had run off to take ringside seats, he turned to her. 'Popcorn? No? An ice-cream maybe? or we could go mad and get a bottle of fizzy lemonade.'

Either he was making fun of her or trying to make light of the situation. She couldn't decide which. He touched her arm lightly. 'Look, you made it clear that you don't want any romantic dealings with me. I get it. I'm sorry if I've upset you in any way. And I promise that I will not try to come on to you. So relax, enjoy the show. Agreed?'

'Agreed – and thank you.'

She was glad he had brought it out in the open, wasn't she? Then why did that small voice that she was trying to stifle ask why she was just a bit disappointed?

CHAPTER FIFTY-EIGHT

The circus programme was entertaining if not riveting. From her seat beside Jason towards the back of the tent, Millie was able to keep an eye on Danny and Maeve and was pleased to see that they were enjoying every minute. Danny seemed to be happier these days as far as she could judge. Everything depended on how he behaved when they returned to school next week. She was hoping that he had simply gone through a bad phase, feeling neglected because she was so preoccupied with running the shop. At least now, thanks to Jason, she had a bit more time for the children and if she was to believe Danny's teacher, that should help to get him back to normal.

She was very conscious of Jason sitting so close beside her. The rows of seats were packed with squealing children and adoring parents and everyone was happily squashing up together.

To her surprise and relief, Jason set out to be entertaining for once, asking her about her sketching, what books she liked to read, her other hobbies. There was so much background noise from the children and indeed from the grown-ups that they could converse in low voices without disturbing anyone around them.

'My grandfather took me fishing when I was about five or six,' he told her. 'I liked that but I must admit I've never taken it up as a hobby. I loved being outdoors. We had braai, (he pronounced it brey) that's South African for barbeque, it's more than just cooking over an open fire, it's a gathering of family and friends. Great fun.'

'That sounds like a lovely childhood.'

'Maybe.' He shrugged slightly. 'A bit lonely when your parents are more interested in business than in you. When Granddad died, I was very lonely. He really was the only one who had time for us children.'

He began to tell her then about his childhood, so different from her own. He had grown up near Cape Town in South Africa, had gone to boarding school in Scotland and to university in London and Dublin. Although he did not say so, she gathered that he came from a very rich family. He did not paint a picture of a cozy family life. It appeared he had been brought up by a series of nannies until he went to boarding school. She remembered now that there had been mention at Fernwood Cottages that he was one of the DeVries mining family. 'Diamond or gold mining. Money to burn, anyway,' as Mrs Donovan put it.

Millie told him briefly about growing up on a housing estate and leaving college to nurse her mother when she became ill. 'I was lucky to find the cottage,' she went on. 'Renting is a nightmare but Fernwood was so reasonable, and I couldn't ask for better neighbours.'

He looked away from her then and she guessed she had hit a nerve. She had not meant to bring up the eviction of the Fernwood Cottages tenants, this was not the time, it had simply evolved from their conversation.

They paused to applaud the trapeze artist and clap enthusiastically with the audience as the clowns filed into the ring.

'You married very young, I think,' Jason said amid the laughter at the antics of the clowns.

'We never actually married, but yes, I suppose I was very young and lonely, too, after mum died,' Millie admitted. 'It didn't work out as you probably know but I'm glad I have Danny and Maeve. They make everything worthwhile.'

'You're doing a great job, anyone can see that. But it's hard to bring up children on your own I should think.'

She flashed him a look but he was watching the clowns as one of them pretended to climb an invisible ladder held by the other two and she could not see his face clearly.

'You're not married?' Normally she would never have asked so personal a question. She wasn't even sure why she had asked.

'I've never been married,' he said. His brows drew together in a frown. 'In fact, I broke up with my fiancée or ex-fiancée to be more exact, before I came here. We'd been planning our wedding and all the while she was cheating on me. I was pretty devastated, I must admit. I needed to be doing something.' Here he stopped short as if realizing that he had said too much, the sentence hung in the air between them.

Millie had never seen him so vulnerable. Never in a million years had she expected him to be so honest, so open. He had always given her the impression that he was self-confident and selfish, a spoiled child grown into a privileged adult. That he was capable of being hurt made him suddenly easier to like.

'That must have been pretty horrible,' she said, then unable to resist, she added 'I don't suppose coming to Fernwood Estate under those circumstances helped very much.'

He turned to look at her. 'Yes, everyone hates the sight of me. I get that. You could also say that I'm learning a lot, learning about Fernwood Cottages and community and all those things that I neither knew nor cared about. Learning about special people.' He smiled at her then and the expression in his eyes caused her to catch her breath.

He reached out and touched her hands where they lay clasped in her lap. 'Don't worry, I'm not coming on to you. I'm just saying what I feel. Don't be mad at me, please. I promise never to bother you again.'

Millie did not know what to say. She most certainly was not mad at him as he put it. She was not sure what she did feel.

The moment was broken by Danny clambering through the seats towards them. 'Maeve's been sick,' he announced loudly.

CHAPTER FIFTY-NINE

Jessica did not want to remember those moments when Ross had kissed her so passionately and she had almost lost herself in the excitement of his kisses. Almost. She had managed to extricate herself gently but firmly from his embrace before things went too far. They stood looking at each other for a long moment.

'I'm sorry,' she said.

He drew a long breath. 'Well, so am I, Jessica.' After a pause he continued. 'Believe me, the last thing I want to do is force you into something you might regret.'

She thought of this now as she scrolled through the description of another luxury hotel in Sardinia and made a note on the pad beside her. It was time – more than time – to make a booking. Owen was due to ring her in a quarter of an hour and she needed his okay and the actual date when he would be home to complete the booking. Once she had booked it, she would feel more secure, more in charge of her emotions, more in charge of her feelings for Ross. That last wildly passionate embrace had unsettled her far more than she wanted to admit. The sooner she was back on firm ground, ready to welcome Owen home for their time away together, the better.

Outside the gloom of a dark evening in early November settled over Fernwood Cottages. She would be glad to get away, to bask in the sun for a few days. As she sat there, waiting for her mobile to ring, she fought the craving for a drink. Since her conversation with Owen she had really tried very hard to stay away from alcohol. It was not easy, especially on a dark, rainy day like today. Her driving licence would be restored next week and she would go for a drive every afternoon, she promised herself. When she was mobile again, she would start looking for a part time job of some kind. It didn't matter what it was: working in a shop or an office, anything that would occupy her time until Owen came home for good. They would go house-hunting together and she would have occupation enough in fitting out their new home.

On the thought her phone rang and she picked it up quickly, eager to get the booking done.

'How are you, Jess?' Owen sounded tired.

'I'm fine. I've been looking at some really nice sunny places we could go to next week. There's one lovely hotel near Alghero and it's not too expensive but we need to be quick, otherwise it'll be gone and there's still the flights to organize.'

He cleared his throat. 'Look Jess, there's been a change of plan. I've been asked to do a series of lectures in Nairobi next week and there will be consultations afterwards. I couldn't say no. There's a big convention being held there which I wasn't aware of until now. I won't bore you with the details but it's a great opportunity for me and for the research programme. We could get really decent funding. You know how badly we need that.'

She cut across him, her voice almost shrill. 'What? What are you saying?'

'I'm saying that I'll be staying on here for another few weeks. I'm sorry, Jess. I was looking forward to a break but this comes first. I know you'll understand.'

'No, I don't understand.' She gripped the phone so tight that her knuckles showed white. 'You promised. I've been so looking forward to this.'

'I know, I know. Look, let's make the best of it. I'll be home for Christmas, that's for sure.'

'And what if another lecture offer comes up? Will I have to spend Christmas on my own just so that you can do your lecturing thing? What do you need family for, if – if we're not important enough to you?'

'Jess, please. I've said I'm sorry. If I could change the way this happened, I would. Please believe me. I miss you. I was looking forward to those few days together.'

'You don't miss me. Not as long as you have your audience in front of you and you can rabbit on about – about physics and molecules and all that super intellectual shit. You didn't really want to come home for a weekend away with me. You told me once already to hold off on the booking, probably while you were looking for a way out of going. Suit yourself. Maybe I'll find someone else to take me to Sardinia.' She hadn't meant to say that, it had just spilled out in her anger and disappointment.

She heard Owen draw a breath. 'Yes,' he said, 'get that fellow Zac to give you a good time. Only don't expect me to be in a hurry to come home.' And he hung up before she could answer.

CHAPTER SIXTY

'And just like that, we split up,' Sherry said, snapping her fingers to emphasize the point.

She was having brunch in one of their favourite cafes with Lara, Bettina and Liz, her three closest friends, on this Saturday morning and had just filled them in on her conversation with Mike.

'That's awful,' Liz said. 'How could he do that after all the time you've been together? What a bastard!'

Bettina, the most practical one of her friends had been stirring her coffee thoughtfully, now she looked up at Sherry. 'You've been very busy lately, Sher. He might have felt left out. I mean, you see more of Zac than you do of Mike, to be honest. Maybe he's jealous, too.'

Sherry found herself blushing, thanks no doubt to Mrs Foley's comments on Zac being the right man for her. 'I have been busy, working my butt off, to be honest. But I do try to keep him in the loop.' She hesitated before continuing, 'As for Zac, well he's a great friend, he's helped me all along with all sorts of things but that's about it. Mike understands that.'

'Has Piers said anything to you about the Board's reaction to your proposal for the Paris office?' Liz asked. 'He wanted it in a hurry and that was weeks ago now, wasn't it?'

'I haven't heard and neither has Vicky. Strange, I'll admit but you never know where you are with Piers.' She looked at the faces of her three closest friends and gave a deep sigh. 'There are times lately when I feel like chucking in the job and looking for something more – what should I call it? – something more fulfilling.'

'This is all because of the break-up with Mike, that crossroads feeling.' Liz reached out and covered Sherry's hand. 'Don't make any wild decisions until you come to terms with that first.'

The others nodded agreement.

'So how do you really, I mean really, feel about the break-up with Mike?' Bettina wanted to know. 'To be honest, Sher, I thought you'd be weeping all over the croissants this morning and here you are looking like you had a great night's sleep and are full of energy.'

Sherry sat back in her chair and regarded her three friends thoughtfully. 'If I'm honest, once I got over the shock of it, I started to feel, oh I dunno, hard to explain but sort of relieved. Relieved that our relationship problems had come to a head or something like that. Relieved that I don't have to make up excuses to Mum about Mike not coming down with me for Christmas. I don't understand it myself, I must admit.'

'What if he changes his mind and wants to make up?' The question came from Liz, who was the romantic one of the friends. 'Would you have him back?'

Sherry thought hard about the question. She had cried herself to sleep that first night. When had her feelings changed? **Had** her feelings changed? She visualized Mike appearing before her, eating humble pie, admitting he was totally wrong and wanting to play a bigger part in her life. Would she welcome him back? Yes or no? If she had asked herself the question last week, she would have known the answer would be a very definite 'yes'. But now? She was not so sure.

'I'd really have to think about that,' she admitted. 'Yes, I still love Mike, but we'd both have to do some compromising.'

'If you really love each other, you'll find a way,' Bettina observed.

CHAPTER SIXTY-ONE

Piers called Sherry into his office on Friday evening. Her pulse quickened at the thought that he was going to offer her the job in Paris. Since her last conversation with Zac, she was unsure what her reaction would be or should be. Should she say yes or no? When she thought about it at night before dropping off to sleep, it seemed like a wonderful opportunity to start a new life without Mike. But when she was showering and dressing in the morning, she found that she was already missing Fernwood Cottages and her neighbours. What would she do without Lady Moll trotting out quotes from obscure works of fiction, Mad Bobby and Jimbo telling her jokes which she had heard a million times before, gossiping with the customers in Mrs Foley's shop? And worst of all, not having Zac popping in for a chat at all hours or sitting in his kitchen eating his home-made lasagne and chatting until the small hours.

'Sit down, Sherry.' Piers waved at the chair on the other side of his desk. It seemed that they were not going to sit at the round table by the window, which would have been the usual procedure.

She took the seat indicated and sat with her hands clasped in her lap, wondering what was coming.

Piers was looking very serious. He cleared his throat and fiddled with his Parker Sonnet Black/Gold fountain pen which he was very proud of. 'I passed on your presentation on opening an office in Paris to the Board,' he began, without looking at her. 'They were impressed, Sherry. I have to say that.' Here he paused for a moment, still not looking at her. The air almost crackled with tension.

'The problem is, Sherry, that a member of the board has discovered that you are leading a protest movement against your landlord. You've been on the radio and you've written a few articles in the local press. The Board are not impressed.'

Sherry stared at him. 'A protest movement? Not exactly. I'm fighting for my neighbours who are being turfed out of their homes, homes that they've been living in for years.'

Piers held up a hand. 'All very laudable I'm sure but the Board do not want the company name to be associated with any protests of any kind.'

'What I'm doing is a private matter,' she said quickly, fighting the sudden lick of anger that coursed through her. 'It has nothing to do with Brooks Business Consultancy, why would it?' It's all done on my own time, not the company's.'

Piers looked at her then, briefly, before returning to playing with his fountain pen. 'It's not that simple, though, is it? Whether you like it or not, you're in the public eye with this protest of yours. The Board member in question heard on his local radio about the Fernwood protests as they are starting to be called. You were mentioned, plus the name of the company you work for, Brooks Business Consultancy. People want to know who you are. It's understandable.'

The blood sang in Sherry's ears, she had to grip her hands tightly together to stop them shaking. This was the last thing she had expected.

'We want you to stop taking part in these protests with immediate effect and not to comment on the situation at Fernwood Estate also with immediate effect.'

Sherry sat in stunned silence. Her mind was a complete blank.

Piers stirred in his chair. 'Do I have your word on that?'

She ran her tongue over dry lips. 'I can't give you my word. I need time to think. I really feel that you and the Board of Directors are – are overreacting and being unreasonable.'

'I'm sorry, Sherry, but unless this matter is cleared up quickly, I'm very doubtful if you will be asked to open and run the Paris office.'

If he had hoped this might cause an immediate change of heart, he was disappointed.

'Is that all?' she asked, her voice shaking now despite all her efforts to keep it level and not show the anger and shock combined, which coursed through her.

Piers got to his feet. 'Yes, that's all, Sherry. You can contact me any time with your answer, but I would seriously advise you for the sake of your career with us, that you abandon this protest business immediately. I'll need your answer for the Board by nine o'clock on Monday morning at the very latest.'

CHAPTER SIXTY-TWO

Following her conversation with Piers, Sherry drove home with her mind in turmoil. What should she do? Give up her well-paid job with Brooks Business Consultancy? That would be madness. The sensible thing to do would be what Piers had advised. There was good reason to believe that if she did so, she would be offered the job in Paris. It would be a huge step up on the promotional ladder. And yet, she found herself worrying over Fernwood Cottages, over Mrs Foley's shop and over The Haven Dogs and Cats Sanctuary. She was the driving force, she acknowledged to herself. Her work experience, her contacts with local Press and radio stations all made publicity for the predicament of the tenants possible. Who else would or could take up the cudgels if she backed out? True, she would not be so severely affected as her neighbours, she earned a good salary and could certainly afford to pay more rent elsewhere. But she loved living here. And besides, she cared about Mrs Foley, Mad Bobby, Jimbo and the rest of them. She could make a success of the shop if it were modernized, she reasoned. This in turn might spare Mrs Foley from losing her home whatever about the others.

When she alighted from her car, she made straight for Zac's cottage. He was always her first port of call in any difficulty and she urgently needed him to listen to what she had to say and calm her simply by his presence. To her disappointment, his door was locked and there was no answer to her knock. She debated sending him a text to ask where he was and then refrained. He had a right to his private life even if he usually told her his plans for the day.

It crossed her mind to ring Mike, but she already knew what his advice would be. She could almost hear his voice. 'Give up your career with Brook Consultancy? You must be mad to even consider it.'

She had until nine o'clock on Monday morning to deliver her answer to Piers. There was time enough to come to a decision.

Without Zac to talk everything over, Sherry found she could not settle to anything. She paced up and down in her little kitchen and occasionally peered through the window in the hope of detecting Zac's battered jeep arriving home. If she took the job in Paris, she would not have his reassuring presence at hand to listen to her, talk things over and make her feel better about everything. If she left Fernwood Cottages, that would be the reality. Only now, with Zac not at home, did she understand how important he was to her. More important than Mike had ever been? Even as she asked herself the question, she batted away the answer. She would get over Mike in time and move on with someone else. Her friendship with Zac was on a different level.

On the thought, her phone beeped. It was Zac. 'Want to come to my gig and maybe help out with serving? They're a bit short staffed tonight.' She could hear voices and laughter in the background.

'Of course. Where are you?'
'McDwyers pub over in Knockraha. Know it?'
'Sort of. I've never been there but I'll find it.'
'Good girl.'

When she put the phone down and went into the bedroom to get ready, she found she was smiling.

'Thanks for coming.' Zac greeted her with a hug. 'They're short staffed, someone called in sick at the last minute, so it would be great if you could help out.'

McDwyers was a small pub and right now it felt to Sherry as if it was full of customers, all talking, laughing, singing along to the music. Zac and his group The Wallows were very popular locally even if they never made the big gigs. She started clearing tables, collecting used glasses and mopping up spills.

'Thank you so much, love,' the owner of the pub, Jer McDwyer said as she helped stack the dishwasher at the end of the evening. 'We couldn't have managed without you.'

'Glad to help,' Sherry said and really meant it. It had been a fun evening, full of banter among the patrons. She had talked to everyone about Fernwood Cottages and Mrs Foley's shop and was pleased at the show of support. Nearly everyone bought something at Mrs Foley's even if they went to Greenfield shopping mall for their major purchases.

Later Zac helped her with the clearing up, stacking chairs and picking up the inevitable rubbish people left behind. 'That was a great night. And we've been asked back for next weekend.'

She laughed happily. 'It was great fun, wasn't it? Maybe we could organize a gig here for funding Mrs Foley's shop.'

'Why not? We'd make good money I would say.' He grinned at her.

She looked around to check that they were on their own in the kitchen at the minute. 'Listen, I wanted to tell you. Piers hauled me in to his office and told me I either had to give up demonstrating and giving radio interviews and press interviews or I might have to give up my job.'

'Really? What an idiot. The demonstrating as he calls it, is your private life. He can't dictate that. What did you tell him?'

'Well, I said more or less the same as you, that it is my private life but apparently one of the Directors heard me being described as an employee of Brooks Business Consultancy on the radio. They don't like it, don't want to be linked with any kind of protest. What do you think I should do, Zac?'

He looked at her thoughtfully. 'Sherry, you have to follow your heart on this one. I can't give you any advice. Only you know what is the right decision for you. I think you know already, don't you?.'

She digested his words in silence for a few minutes. Follow your heart, he had said. Wasn't this what she had been telling herself since her conversation with Piers?

She drew a deep breath. 'I've decided that I'll hand in my notice on Monday. I never did want to go to Paris, in my heart of hearts I didn't. I know that now. It doesn't matter what happens here, whether we're successful or not. I'll find another job. And I'll keep fighting for the Fernwood Cottages people.'

'If you're sure that that is what you want to do, then I'd say go for it.' He gave her a quick hug.

There was another silence between them for a minute or two. Zac was deep in thought. Finally, he spoke as if weighing his words.

'I heard you laughing a lot tonight,' he said slowly, 'and you certainly look relaxed despite all the fun and games at Brooks Consultancy. Have you sorted things out about Mike?'

She had not thought about Mike tonight. Her first thoughts had been to tell Zac all that had happened with Piers. Just getting it out into the open made a huge difference and she could not find a better listener than Zac.

Standing there at the kitchen sink in McDwyers' pub, she had what could only be described as an epiphany. She looked at Zac, really looked at him, as if seeing him for the first time. Why had she been so blind? He was her soul mate; he always had been if she had only seen it before. How could she have been so blinded by Mike and his pseudo charm? Mike who never put himself out for anyone. Who enjoyed the benefits of their relationship but did not want to commit himself. Without realizing it, she had always put Zac first, his good opinion, indeed his opinion on anything held more sway with her than anybody else's. Sight of him always cheered her and made her feel that everything would be all right. She had taken him for granted all along and he had been happy to be there for her in the background, through thick and thin, despite all her shortcomings. Deep down she had known it, had refused to face it.

Looking back, she acknowledged that one of the reasons she had come to her decision about the Paris project was that she did not want to move away from Zac, however much she had wrapped it up as loyalty to her Fernwood Cottage neighbours. Even if they had to move out, they could still find an apartment to share, she had reasoned.

Zac was waiting for an answer.

'Yes,' she said, holding his gaze. 'I have sorted Mike out. I'm only just beginning to realize that he was a figment of my romantic imagination.'

Zac threw his head back and gave a hearty laugh. 'That sounds like something out of a romance novel, only I know you never read romance novels or that's what you told me.'

'I don't know what it sounds like, but it's the truth. I've done a lot of thinking and I feel better, so much better without Mike.'

'Are you serious?'

'Absolutely serious.'

His face lit up. 'I can't say I'm sorry. You were always too good for him but then I guess I'm prejudiced.' He hesitated a moment.' We've always understood each other. Do you think that – later on when you're ready for it – the two of us could maybe have a chance of getting together, make a go of it?' He spoke so softly she barely caught the words.

She turned so that she could face him. 'Zac, I think I'm ready now only I've been too completely stupid to see it.'

She heard him give a gasp of surprise. 'Sherry? Really?'

The next moment she felt herself drawn into his arms, his mouth seeking hers in a long kiss. It felt like coming home.

CHAPTER SIXTY-THREE

Jessica's hand shook at little as she set the glass of gin down on the coffee table. Her head was starting to spin but she did not want to stop, to sober up and face what had happened between herself and Owen last night. He had put work first yet again, she thought bitterly. He might not even be home for Christmas. A vision of herself on Christmas day sitting alone over a toasted sandwich brought the tears to her eyes, even though she knew she was being overdramatic. For some years now, her parents went on a fourteen-day cruise to the Caribbean with some friends over the holiday period. Her brother and his family lived in Australia. They would all be more than delighted if she opted to spend Christmas with them. However, the thought of having to face their unspoken questions as to why Owen was not there for the festive season, of having to pretend she was happy with the situation – she would never admit to anyone, friend or family that she was hurt and humiliated – was more than she wanted to endure.

The buzz of her mobile indicating a WhatsApp call almost went unnoticed for a minute or two before she picked up. 'Hello?' Her voice sounded slurred even to her own ears.

'Jess? Are you all right?' It was Ross.

'Never better.' She couldn't keep the anger out of her voice as she articulated the words.

'Hey, what's going on?' He sounded genuinely concerned.

She forced a laugh which came out all wrong. 'I'm okay just a bit –She had been about to say 'lonely' but changed it to 'disappointed' instead.

He drew an audible breath. 'Sit tight. I'm on my way.'

He signed off before she could answer. The thought of him made her pulse quicken. She emptied her glass in one gulp and then went to brush her teeth and get ready. She had been sitting in her pyjamas since she got out of bed this morning. She stood under the shower for a few minutes – it would not take Ross long to get here and she wanted to be ready when he did – finding comfort in the feel of the warm water washing over her. From her wardrobe she chose one of her favourite outfits, designer slacks and a top in a soft filmy material in midnight blue which matched her eyes. She studied her reflection in the bathroom mirror as she applied make-up. Her eyes looked puffy, she thought. That was partially from crying last night but also maybe from the alcohol she had been consuming. Her head swam as she walked through to the kitchen and poured herself a glass of water.

She was standing at the kitchen cupboard with the bottle of gin in her hand and debating whether she should have another glass when Ross knocked at the door and walked in. She hastily put the bottle down on the kitchen counter as he came up to her and took her in his arms, holding her tight before letting her go.

'You look beautiful,' he said. 'Too beautiful to be as sad as you sounded on the phone.'

She half turned away and put a hand on the kitchen counter to steady herself. 'Oh, I'm all right really. It's just – it's just that Owen won't be able to get home for our few days in Sardinia, that's all. I'd been so looking forward to getting away.'

She heard his swift intake of breath, then he put his hands on her shoulders and turned her to face him. 'Let's do it, Jess.

Let's go away for a few days. The offer of that villa in the South of France is still open. What do you say?'

'All right.' Jessica was never sure afterwards if it was the gin talking or her anger at Owen or even that she fancied Ross a bit and was flattered by his attentions. It was most likely a combination of all three. 'All right. Let's do it.'

'Oh you darling.' He did kiss her then, wild and passionate, until she pushed him away with hands that shook.

'Not now, Ross. I – I need time. Please understand.'

He smiled down at her. 'You're right. Let's save this for our first night at the Villa Mirabelle.'

CHAPTER SIXTY-FOUR

Jessica did not know what would have happened next despite Ross' words 'let's save this for our first night at the Villa Mirabelle', if his mobile had not chimed to indicate an incoming call. With a muttered curse he had checked who the call was from and then with an apologetic wave of his hand, had turned away from her, speaking in a low voice with whoever was on the other end of the phone.

Jessica took the opportunity to put away the bottle of gin. Her mouth must have tasted of alcohol, she thought in embarrassment. She was debating popping into the bathroom and brushing her teeth again when Ross ended his call and turned his attention back to her.

'Sorry about that,' he said, 'a stupid mix-up at the salon about some stuff we ordered. I have to get it sorted, I'm afraid.'

He sounded irritated, or maybe angry was a better description, even if he was trying to appear normal. Somehow, she did not believe that the call had come from his salon. A girlfriend maybe? Why not? After all I have a husband in the background, she told herself.

'Darling, I have to go,' he came and put his hands on her shoulders, kissing her lightly on the lips before releasing her. 'Maybe it's just as well or we might have got ahead of our honeymoon.'

When Ross had left, Jessica sat down and cried without really knowing why. She took out the bottle of gin and slowly drank most of it, not bothering to make herself anything to eat. Had she really agreed to go away with Ross? Was she glad or sorry that they were interrupted by that phone call? She wasn't sure. She felt as if she were drifting without being able to control what was happening.

Next morning, she lay in bed, her head throbbing from last night's drinking, and tried to envisage what it would be like to be with Ross. Thoughts of Owen finding out intruded on the images of herself and Ross basking by the pool at the Villa Mirabelle. She recalled that kiss last night and what he had said. 'let's save this for our first night at the Villa Mirabelle.' She had never slept with anyone except Owen and the idea now filled her with panic. Ross was a sophisticated man-of-the-world whereas she was really just a simple housewife. How would it be with him? Would she measure up to all the women he doubtless had before her?

She started up in fright when her mobile rang. Was it Ross with plans already in place for their South of France affair? She wasn't ready to face that, not yet anyway.

The voice on the other end was Owen's. 'How are you, Jen?'

She swallowed hard. When people said their mouth felt like the bottom of a birdcage, she knew what that meant now. 'Owen,' she croaked. 'You're ringing me early aren't you? It's only –'she squinted at the time on her phone. It was a quarter to twelve. She must have slept for much longer than she realized. God knows what the time was where Owen was located.

'Are you all right? You sound a bit hoarse.'

'I'm okay.' To her annoyance, her words were still a bit slurred.

'You've been drinking.' She could hear the anger in his voice. 'What are you up to, Jen?'

If you only knew, she thought. 'I'm not up to anything. Why?'

He gave a loud, exasperated sigh. 'I know you, Jen. Something's going on. You've been drinking, haven't you? Have you been painting the town red with Zac?'

'I most certainly have not. I haven't seen Zac in days, not since he returned my car for me, if you must know.'

'Jen, listen to me. I know you're lonely. I know you're disappointed about us not going away as we planned. But drinking doesn't help.'

'Don't preach at me,' she snapped. 'You're not the one who's hanging around with nothing to do and no place to go. You're enjoying yourself over there away from me. You can't blame me if -' She broke off.

'If what? You're cheating on me, is that what you're saying?'

'Supposing I am? You don't really care, do you, all you think about is your lecture programme.'

There was silence at the other end for a full minute, then Owen said, very softly. 'I love you, Jen. Nothing is ever going to change how I feel about you. I want you to know that. But if you've found someone else, well, I guess it's curtains for our marriage.'

She started to cry in earnest then but before she could say anything, he had hung up.

CHAPTER SIXTY-FIVE

'I'm allowed home on Friday,' Mrs Foley said, sounding chirpier than Millie had heard her in a long time. 'I'll have to use a walking stick and go to physical therapy and all that, but they said I could go home.'

Zac had driven Millie to The Laurels and was to collect her again later on while Mad Bobby and Jimbo managed the shop. The children were back at school after the Halloween break and Mrs Donovan was to collect them. Millie had not seen Jason since their visit to the circus. She was glad, she told herself, and yet part of her wanted badly to see him.

'That's the best news.' Millie said now, although she wondered if Mrs Foley would be able to look after herself. Would she even manage to negotiate the steep stairs leading to her living quarters over the shop? The best thing would be to convert one of the back rooms into a bedroom. She would talk to Zac and Sherry about arranging this at short notice.

As if reading her thoughts, Mrs Foley patted her hands. 'I'm getting someone in to look after me, a kind of housekeeper not a minder – I'm not bad enough for that yet. They told me it's all arranged. So you needn't worry, love. I'll still need you to help in the shop, at least for the time being, if that's all right.'

Millie wanted to ask who had arranged for a housekeeper but then decided against it. Clearly there was enough money available for The Laurels and then for a housekeeper, wherever it came from. Although Mrs Foley would not be up to managing the shop for a long time to come, the prospect of being back home was already having a very positive effect. She sat up straighter in her chair and there was colour in her face. But how much longer would she be able to call the shop and Fernwood Cottages "home"?

'Mrs Foley will be home tomorrow,' Millie told the meeting at the shop on the Thursday evening. 'I thought we might have a little tea party for her to welcome her back.'

There were murmurs of approval.

'Brilliant,' Sherry said. 'Let's do a big bash and invite the local media. It will be good publicity for the shop, too.'

Everyone started talking at once and it took a little while to get the meeting back on track. Lady Moll was already totting up how many cakes she would bake. Mad Bobby and Jimbo were offering their services, too. Sherry managed to convince them that she would do all the organizing and would call on them individually for any help needed.

'Have we heard anything further on our terminations of tenancy stuff?' Mrs Donovan wanted to know when everyone had quietened down again.

'Afraid nothing positive,' Sherry said. 'The letting agents simply acknowledged receipt of our solicitor's letter and said they would reply in due course. Our solicitor is not very hopeful that anything can be done.'

'Did I see you talking to DeVries a couple of days ago, Zac?' Mrs Donovan asked. Very little happened in the neighbourhood that she did not know about.

'Yes, you did,' Zac said, aware no doubt that all eyes had turned on him. 'He came into Mrs Foley's shop. I asked him what was going on about the cottages and he said his solicitor was handling everything and that he was going to be away. I got the impression that he's moving on. So I'd guess nothing's changed.'

'Tell you what, we'll invite him to Mrs Foley's tea party,' Sherry said. 'If he comes, it will be the perfect opportunity to ask him how plans are progressing and the media will be there too, to witness what's going on.'

CHAPTER SIXTY-SIX

During the long sleepless night, Jessica had gone over everything in her mind. Her loneliness, the feeling that Owen didn't understand or care, her enjoyment of Ross's company. She had got out of bed at three a.m. and gone into the kitchen where she had stood for a few minutes in front of the cupboard where she kept the bottle of gin. Steeling herself, she had opened the door, taken the bottle and poured the contents down the sink, running the tap for ten minutes to get rid of the smell of alcohol.

If she expected this action to make her feel better, she was disappointed. What she felt was panic, she could feel the thump of her heart down to her fingertips. Well, she had burned her boats. She would not be able to buy a new supply of gin until the shops opened later this morning. She paced up and down in the kitchen, pulling her dressing gown tightly around her against the chill of early morning. Outside the rain splashed down, adding to the gloom and doom.

She made herself a mug of coffee and sat down on the sofa to drink it, her thoughts whirling like snowflakes in a blizzard. How could she have ever thought of cheating on Owen? Owen who loved her, would always love her. Not only that, he was ready to take responsibility for her, for the children, for the family. Yes, he was devoted to his work as lecturer but wasn't that infinitely better than if he hated his job? And whose fault was it if she did not have anything to occupy her? She could have joined her neighbours in helping out at Mrs Foley's shop. She could have offered to drive Millie's children to school. She could even have tried to keep up her acquaintance with Samantha at the fitness centre.

Owen's words came back to haunt her. 'if you've found someone else, well, I guess it's curtains for our marriage'. If they did break up it would be all her fault. It was brought home to her then that she could not face a life without him.

Ross phoned her as she was eating her lonely breakfast of tea and toast.

'We're all set. I've booked the flights for Monday afternoon. Weather forecast is for warm and sunny. Bring your bikini.'

Jessica's knuckles showed white as she gripped her phone. He sounded so happy, so pleased with himself, that she felt sorry for what she was going to tell him.

'Ross, please don't hate me, but I can't, I just can't.'

'Can't? Can't what? Can't have some fun? What's got into you this morning?'

'Nothing's got into me, as you put it. It's just – oh I suppose I realized that I can't cheat on Owen. I'm really really sorry, Ross. I've enjoyed the times with you but it has to end here and now.'

'We did plan to end it after we went to the South of France, remember? What's giving you cold feet?'

'I've done a lot of thinking.' This conversation was proving harder than she had envisaged.

'I've done a lot of thinking, too, Jess. I've been thinking about making love to you on the beach, in the moonlight, how good we'll be together. You can't deny me that.' Before she could frame an answer, he went on, 'I'm on my way over to you, Jess. I think you need to think some more about this. Hang in there.'

Ross was so convinced of his own charm, she realized, so confident that he was the perfect lover, that he could not believe that any woman would say no to him. She felt a flick of anger run through her. He had never tried to see things from her point of view, had never understood her conflict about cheating on her husband. He just wanted to go to bed with her, to have a good time and then walk away when Owen came home. That was not the kind of person she was. Maybe it was my fault for giving that impression, she thought. Maybe I didn't see the real me in all of this.

'Don't come over, Ross. I don't think we should see each other again.'

There was a pause during which he did some thinking as was shown by his next words. 'If that's the way you want it, good luck to you. I'd have given you a few days to remember at the Villa Mirabelle. You're loss, my sweet.'

CHAPTER SIXTY-SEVEN

It was a long day, dark and dank as November days often were. Jessica fought off the temptation to get in the car and drive to Greenfields shopping centre to buy a bottle of gin. Twice she picked up her car keys only to put them back again. If there was anything to be learned from the fiasco with Ross it was that she must learn to stand on her own two feet, to stop drinking, find a life for herself. She researched her nearest Alcoholics Anonymous group and was determined to go to their next meeting on the coming Thursday night. Tomorrow she would go to see Sherry and volunteer to help with the party for Mrs Foley which all the neighbours were talking about. And after Christmas, she would see if there was some further education course that she could enroll in. She would ask Millie if she could help out in the shop. And she would make an effort to get to know her neighbours.

By the time night fell, she was exhausted but feeling more contented in herself than for a long time. It would be an uphill battle but she could make it.

Jessica was woken out of a deep sleep some time during the night by the sound of the front door closing and the clunk as if someone had set down a heavy bag of some sort in the kitchen. She sat bolt upright in bed, waves of panic washing over her.

There was a tap on the bedroom door and in the dim light she made out the figure of a man standing there.

'Jess? Are you awake?'

'Owen.' She was out of bed and running towards him with outstretched arms. 'Owen.'

He caught her and pulled her tight against him, his face buried in her hair. She said the first thing that came into her head. 'How – why - did you get here?'

He relaxed his hold and peered down at her in the dimness of the bedroom. 'What's going on, Jess? I had to find out.'

It was like opening a floodgate, all her pent up emotions spilled out, her words tripping over themselves. She told him everything, about Ross, the job she didn't get, the loneliness, the feeling of being ignored. In her own defence, she told him that she was giving up drinking and would actively look at ways to improve her life.

'I've been acting like a selfish spoiled brat,' she said slowly. 'I've ignored the neighbours here, yes, even nosy Mrs Donovan. I could have tried helping out at Mrs Foley's shop or looking after Millie's kids now and again. Instead, I just sat around feeling sorry for myself.'

When she started speaking, he had taken a step away from her. He listened in silence, arms folded across his chest, not attempting to interrupt. She tried to see his expression but he had his back to the light from the kitchen and she could not see his face in the dimness of the bedroom. He seemed very far away, very distant from her. Was this then the end of their marriage? Was it too late to salvage anything from the wreckage?

'Here,' he reached for her dressing gown where it hung over a chair. 'You'll get cold standing around like that.'

She put on the dressing gown obediently. When she spoke, her voice was husky with unshed tears. "I swear to you that nothing happened with Ross. Yes, I suppose I was flattered, but that's no excuse. I should never have gone out with him in the first place.'

What was he thinking, why didn't he speak to her?

'I've been so stupid and selfish, just thinking of myself,' she said forcing herself to go on even if she did not know what to say, how to tell him how much she hated herself. 'I suppose I can't blame you if you –' her voice broke.

Her words hung in the air between them. It seemed an age until he spoke.

'If you'd asked me yesterday, I'd most likely have said that no I can't forgive you,' he said slowly. 'I've done a lot of thinking since then. There isn't much else to do when you're waiting around for flight connections. But I can't help it, Jess. You're part of my life. I love you. I can't leave you, no matter what you did.'

She saw then that he was exhausted, that she had overlooked the fact that he had been through his own private hell. Anger at herself spurted through her. How selfish she had been, how thoughtless.

'You mean, we have a chance?'

She saw the glimmer of a smile. 'I've been the worst sort of husband, too tied up with my work to see what was under my nose. I didn't even try to understand that you're lonely with the kids being away and everything. We've both been more than a bit stupid.' He held out his arms. 'Come here, Jess. If we both try hard, we can fix this.'

CHAPTER SIXTY-EIGHT

It was two weeks to Christmas. The weather had taken a turn for the better with bright sunny days, cold but with clear blue skies. Danny and Maeve were wildly excited about the coming feast. Millie wished she could share their enthusiasm. There was an ache in her heart that had not been there until a few short weeks ago. If someone had told her that Jason DeVries was the cause, she would not have believed them. But so it was.

Looking back, she began to realize that she had fought the attraction to Jason almost from the start. After all, he was responsible for turning her and her neighbours out of their homes. How could she ever have any feelings for him? She had hardened her heart against his attempts to help her, had made it plain to him that she did not want his attentions. But bit by bit he had got through her defences.

Why was it, when she was now safe from those attentions, that she began to admit to herself that she liked him, that she wanted to get to know him better? She felt that he liked her. But perhaps she had imagined his interest. Mrs Donovan had been peeved because Millie seemed to be getting friendly with the enemy, as she would see it, but neither she nor Mrs Foley had seriously considered that there could be anything romantic in the relationship. Mrs Donovan would normally be the first to bring it up. It would be high on her list of interesting gossip.

In any case, how could a relationship ever work? Jason was throwing all of them out of their homes. And even if everything was normal between them, why would he choose her? She was way out of his sphere. He would have his pick of glamorous, rich women to choose from. This last thought was perhaps the most depressing.

It was too late now, anyway, since he was not coming back. Sherry had taken over the evenings in the shop in his place. She had quit her job and was now almost full time there, which in turn meant that Millie was able to resume her cleaning jobs. To everyone's surprise, Jessica had come forward to offer her services and now dropped the children off at school and collected them in the afternoons, so that Millie was able to take on a few more cleaning jobs in the area, thus enabling her to put more money away for when she had to leave Fernwood Cottages.

Danny and Maeve missed Jason almost as much as she did and nearly every day she had to parry their questions about where he was and why he didn't drive them to school. The neighbourhood in general did not comment on his absence. For once, she thought Mrs Donovan, always the first with everybody's news, very backward in telling her neighbours where Jason was and when he was coming back. She gathered that Sherry had sent him an invitation to the welcome home party for Mrs Foley.

'A party here? Won't be posh enough for him,' Mrs Donovan had sniffed. 'He soon got tired of us, didn't he? I see the workmen are up at the Big House. Looks like he's polishing it up to put it on the market along with our cottages.'

He had not replied to Sherry's invitation, as Mrs Donovan hastened to tell her.

'Not his cup of tea,' she said, with another of her sniffs. 'We don't want him anyway.'

Meanwhile, preparations for the party were in full swing. There would be a marquee which was to be set up in the spacious garden at the rear of the shop. Zac had volunteered to man the barbeque, Lady Moll was planning to bake all kinds of cakes day and night and Sherry had managed to engage a magician and a troupe of clowns, together with a suitable tent, for the entertainment of the children. Several local suppliers donated prizes for the raffle that would be held at the end of the afternoon. With the weather forecast promising a chilly but sunny day, everything seemed set for an entertaining afternoon.

CHAPTER SIXTY-NINE

On the Monday before the party, the tenants all received a letter from Jason DeVries requesting them to attend a meeting at the Big House on the Thursday night to "discuss the current situation".

Millie turned over the envelope in her hands before opening it. Her heart sank as she read the contents. There were still some months left before their termination of tenancy notice expired, so why was it even necessary to meet? At the same time, her heart gave a little flutter at the thought of seeing him again.

'I betcha he wants us out earlier than he said,' was Mrs Donovan's comment.

On the Thursday evening, Millie dressed with more care than usual and applied light make up, fussing over her appearance in front of the bedroom mirror. She did not want it to look as if she had done herself up specially for the meeting with Jason, even if, in fact she had. She was looking forward to seeing him again and dreading it at the same time. What would he have to say to them all? Was Mrs Donovan right and he was anxious that they move out earlier than stipulated? Would this be the last time she would see him?

Mrs Donovan walked up with her. Podge had elected to look after Millie's children while they were gone. Millie had never been inside Fernwood House. The front door was open but there was no sign of Jason. They stepped into the high-ceilinged hall with its two wide, curving staircases leading to a landing. Portraits of former owners and of hunting scenes and landscapes decorated the walls. The place had an air of shabby gentility. There was a faint smell of fresh paint emanating from the upper floors where the workmen were no doubt starting to re-decorate.

Millie stood looking about her with Mrs Donovan at her side until Jason appeared and led them into a small sitting room off the hall. The rest of the cottage tenants were already seated. Zac and Sherry had driven Jimbo and Mad Bobby, while Lady Moll had walked up on her own. Mrs Foley had elected to stay at home. 'I'm not able for them kinds of things,' she had told Millie. 'Sure I'll find out soon enough what he's planning now.'

Jason took up a position in front of them by the open fireplace where a log fire crackled.

'Thank you all for coming,' he said, his eyes resting on Millie for a moment. 'I know you have been worried and upset by all that has happened and I wanted to tell you that I am truly sorry.'

He had their complete attention now. An apology was unexpected, but it did not solve anything as far as they were concerned.

Jason seemed to understand that now was not the time for a flowery speech of some sort. 'I just wanted to let you all know in advance, that your notice of termination has been revoked. In other words, you can stay on as tenants. You will get a letter from my lawyers to this effect within the next few days.'

There was a moment of stunned silence and then complete uproar broke out with everyone talking at once. This was the last thing anyone had expected. Millie clasped her hands tightly in her lap, feeling as if she might fall or float away into space. She didn't have to find a new place to live, she and the children could stay in the cottage. She could see the surprise turning to relief and joy on the faces of the others.

Jason looked around the room, his eyes resting on Millie again as if willing her to meet his gaze. She felt the colour burning her cheeks. Her heart was so full that she felt if she looked at him, she would betray her feelings and until she had got herself under control, she was afraid of what he could read in her face. She turned away towards Mrs Donovan. Mrs Donovan, in fact, was at a loss for words for probably the first time in her life.

'If you have any questions, I'd be happy to answer them,' Jason went on. 'There is no change to the terms of your tenancies. Everything will return to be as it was.'

'Why are you doing this now?' Lady Moll was the first to recover from the surprise.

'That's not easy to answer,' Jason told her. 'To be honest, I never intended spending so much time here. I don't know when I realized what a wonderful community spirit you have, how you all help each other. I have never experienced anything like it. The next stage was to ask myself what I should do. I had a buyer who had put in an offer. I had no other ties to the place. Why would I want to stay here?' Here he paused and again he looked at Millie. 'Something made me change my mind. Made me realize that this is where I want to be.'

The rest of the meeting was all a blur as far as Millie was concerned. His words echoed in her head. 'Something made me change my mind' he had said. He had tried to catch her eye, but she had looked away, signalling that she did not want to know. Why oh why did I do that? she asked herself. She now bitterly regretted not giving him any sign of encouragement. She had burned her boats as far as Jason DeVries was concerned. The overwhelming relief at being able to stay in the cottage could not assuage the ache in her heart.

CHAPTER SEVENTY

When Jason had finished answering questions and everyone was standing around, going but not going, Sherry turned to Zac who stood beside her. 'Wow, what do you make of that? I have never been so flabbergasted in my life.'

'Me neither. I've been pinching myself ever since he told us.' Zac's grin spread all over his face. 'The last thing anyone expected isn't it? Look at Mad Bobby, he's about to fall on the floor.'

'Do you believe what he said about being sort of influenced by our community spirit as he called it?'

Zac shrugged. 'Who knows? We'll never understand how the rich people think, now will we? The main thing is he did change his mind and will let us stay on. Happy days!'

Sherry looked around her at her neighbours. 'I still can't get over it. Wait until Mrs Foley hears. She will be so happy and relieved, too.' She clasped her hands together .'This has to be like a fairy tale coming true. I could kiss Jason DeVries.'

'Here's your chance,' Zac laughed as Jason walked up to where they were standing.

'Can I have a word with you?' he asked, addressing Sherry. He looked very serious, grim almost, she thought.

'Of course.' She wondered what was coming. Had he decided to make an exception on the lease of her cottage?

'I've been doing a lot of thinking,' he said. 'You've made a fantastic job of modernizing Mrs Foley's shop. I know a lot needs to be done yet but you already transformed it.' Here he was interrupted by Lady Moll wishing everyone good -night.

'Thank you,' Sherry managed to say before he continued.

'The shop needs someone to do the marketing and planning. If Mrs Foley agrees – and I see no reason why she should not – I will finance the role of executive if you agree to take on the job. In addition, I will provide the financing for the improvements.' He waved a dismissive hand as Sherry opened her mouth to speak. 'Don't worry, I'll take a share of the profits, so I'll be expecting a lot of hard work from you.' This with a smile at her.

If Sherry was surprised by the turn of events earlier tonight, she was even more surprised now. She could only stare at him as she slowly absorbed what he had just said.

When she had handed in her notice, Piers had been both surprised and angry.

'You're making a big mistake,' he said. 'Jobs like this aren't thick on the ground. The Paris office job, which of course Brooks intended offering you, would have done wonders for your career.'

Was he right, she sometimes wondered, even if she did not regret her decision. Since leaving Brooks Business Consulting she had been looking for a position which answered her need for challenge. Suitable positions were not so easy to come by as she was learning, having applied here and there for a promising looking job only to be rejected without even an interview.

'You're bound to get something,' Zac always consoled her. 'These things take time. You're a highly efficient, intelligent woman. The right job will come along.'

Jason's proposal of putting her in charge of the shop was exactly suited to her wishes. Working with Mrs Foley would be a pleasure.

'Think it over and let me know,' Jason said. 'You don't have to decide now.

'I can safely say that I'll take the job,' she said, a smile in her voice. 'I know I can make a difference. And Mrs Foley keeping the shop is just the perfect solution.'

'Good. I'll have your contract drawn up next week.'

Later that evening, Sherry texted her three best friends on WhatsApp. *You know, when Zac and I got together, I thought I couldn't be happier,* she wrote. *'Then the bombshell tonight about letting us stay in our cottages and if that wasn't enough, I'll be working with Mrs Foley on running the shop. I could never have foreseen any of this. Happy days.*

CHAPTER SEVENTY-ONE

On the day of the party, Millie walked down to Mrs Foley's with the children early in the morning. She was to man the shop for a few hours before it was closed for the party. Mrs Foley was up and dressed already when she got there.

'This is marvellous news that we can stay in Fernwood Cottages,' the old lady said. 'I don't know when I've felt happier.'

'We're all over the moon,' Millie said. 'None of us expected anything like that.'

'Whatever made him change his mind, we can only be glad he did.'

Millie did not have anything to say on that subject. 'Everyone is delighted that you'll be able to keep the shop,' she said. 'And it's good to see you looking so well today.'

'You're all too good,' the old lady said, wiping a tear from the corner of her eye.

'You deserve it,' Millie told her as she hung up her jacket and prepared to serve customers. 'We're so glad to have you back.'

'You know, I was always wondering who paid my hospital bill and got me into The Laurels,' Mrs Foley went on, speaking in a low voice as if afraid of being overheard although the shop was empty. 'I thought it might be the neighbours here. I knew it couldn't be my sister. She doesn't have two pennies to rub together.'

Millie was busy sorting the daily newspapers into their respective piles on the display stand and was only half listening.

'Would you believe it was Jason DeVries?' Mrs Foley said. 'And he never said a word about it.'

Millie jumped in surprise and a stack of newspapers went sliding to the floor. 'Jason DeVries? Are you sure?'

Mrs Foley chuckled. 'You're just as surprised as me, love. I couldn't believe it. I only found it out by accident because someone in the office at The Laurels sent a receipt addressed to me instead of to him. I rang them up, you see, to find out what it was all about. I mean, I don't really know DeVries and I thought it might be some mistake.'

Millie stared at her. 'It really was him?'

'Oh yes, love. And he's paying for me to have a carer if you can call it that. It's all been set up and paid for, they tell me.' She paused a moment. 'I hope he does come to the party today so that I can thank him. But now, don't mention it to anybody else. He asked that it be kept quiet.'

Millie went back to stacking the newspapers without knowing what she was doing. Why would Jason do such a thing? Did he feel guilty about all the worry he had caused? When he apologized last night at the meeting, he had sounded sincere. Of course he was rich and could afford to be generous. He had helped her too, driving the children to school and driving her to the hospital to see Mrs Foley. Yes, he had a way of looking at her which made her insides melt but she had clearly signalled that his attentions were not wanted. Even if he did show up at the party this afternoon and even if she did succeed in speaking to him, it was very doubtful that he would want to renew his interest in her. 'Don't worry, I'm not going to come on to you,' he had said at the circus.

She gave a gusty sigh. She had misjudged him and now when she could acknowledge that and confess to herself that she really would like to get to know him better, it was too late. Despite the excitement around her and despite Mrs Foley's happy face, she had never felt so miserable in her entire life.

CHAPTER SEVENTY-TWO

A huge crowd turned out for Mrs Foley's party. Everyone for miles around or so it seemed, descended on Fernwood Cottages. Maeve and Danny's schoolfriends all came with parents and in some cases grandparents in tow.

Zac slaved over the barbecue, barely keeping up with demand. Jessica manned the table where teas and coffees were served. After spending a few days with her at the cottage, Owen had had to return to Africa to resume his lecture tour. He would be home for Christmas and the children had both promised to be there, too. Selina's proposed trip to Vienna with her girlfriend had fallen through and she was more than happy to join the family party. Before he left again, Owen had booked them all into a hotel in Obertauern in Austria. 'Snow and log fires,' he had said, 'a perfect Christmas setting.'

This time, when she said goodbye to him, she did not feel so lonely or abandoned as on other occasions.

People greeted Jessica with a smile as she served teas and coffees, stopping to chat to her. She was starting to get to know her neighbours, she admitted to herself, and for the first time in a very long time, she was beginning to feel at home here among them. She even chatted to Mad Bobby and Jimbo when they came over to get a hot drink.

'I've been off the booze for two weeks,' Jimbo confessed to her as she poured him a mug of tea, seeming to think he owed an explanation as to why he was drinking something non-alcoholic. 'I might stay off now. I never felt better.'

Inwardly, Jessica winced at his words. Although she would never have thought of it in the same terms as Jimbo, she was 'off the booze' herself and attending a self-help group ever since Owen had paid his surprise visit and she, too, felt considerably better for it. Only now did she really understand what a destructive road she had been on. She gave Jimbo her warmest smile. Instead of looking down on him, which she had been doing in the past, she felt a kinship between them. Who knew what his demons were? She would never judge anybody again, she vowed.

Sherry was giving interviews to the local radio station while reporters from various newspapers scribbled in their notebooks as she extolled the necessity of having a local shop in the area.

When she had told her friends that she was happier than she had ever been in her life, it was no exaggeration. Zac would come home with her for Christmas. There was no need to make up excuses any more for Mike's non-appearances. She was looking forward to introducing Zac to the family. Her mother did not fully approve, she knew, although she was happy for her. If Zac had a job as executive in some upmarket firm, she would have been happier. Sherry, on the other hand, was sick of ambition and high-flying managers. She was more than content to be with Zac, to have a much smaller income than she was used to, and to be able to call Fernwood Cottages home. Following an agreement with Jason DeVries, they were planning on building an extension to Zac's cottage.

'We'll make it state of the art,' Zac had said with a laugh. 'Big enough for five kids at least.'

Sherry had laughed, too. 'Sounds wonderful. A proper kitchen maybe and a hallway. Wow. Not sure about the five kids though. Two might be more than enough.'

Mrs Foley did not want to be interviewed but allowed a photographer to take her picture and then, in the end, spoke to the reporters about her shop and how long she had lived at Fernwood Cottages. She was clearly overwhelmed by the number of people who came to shake her hand and welcome her home.

'I have the very best neighbours,' she said, smiling around at them all. 'I wouldn't want to live anywhere else.'

Mrs Donovan won the first prize for the raffle – a huge hamper of Christmas goodies. 'Ye'll all have to come round for tea,' she told them as she inspected it, 'sure Podge and meself couldn't eat all that.'

'You're on,' Zac said with a laugh. 'Sherry and I want to celebrate our engagement, and we might as well do it in style at your place, Mrs D.'

'Congratulations to the two of ye,' Mrs Donovan joined in the laugh. 'I wondered when you'd get round to it.'

Jason DeVries did not come to the party. Millie kept an eye out for him despite being busy supervising the children's activities in the tent dedicated to them. There was no sign of him, however. She had been steeling herself to meet him and going over in her mind how to thank him for all he had done and was still doing for Mrs Foley. Now, it looked as if she needn't have bothered.

CHAPTER SEVENTY-THREE

It was two days before Christmas. The weather had been mild and rainy all week but today the wind had changed direction and a few icy flakes were floating through the air.

At Fernwood Cottages, all was quiet. Sherry and Zac had gone to her parents for the holiday. Jessica and her family had taken off for their holiday in Austria. Lady Moll and the Donovans went to visit respective family members as they did every year. This year, on Sherry's advice, Mrs Foley had closed the shop until New Year and she and her sister had headed to Killarney for Christmas. 'Sure, I'm getting very grand,' she had said with a laugh. Sherry would open up the shop again for New Year.

As in the past, Millie would have Mad Bobby and Jimbo for Christmas dinner and they would all watch a Christmas film afterwards while Maeve and Danny played with their new toys.

Millie shivered as she stood at the bus stop near Greenwoods shopping centre. She set down her heavy shopping bags and checked her watch. The bus was due in about fifteen minutes. It was cold standing here but hardly worth while to trek back into the warmth of the shopping centre.

Maeve and Danny had been invited to a friend of Danny's to celebrate his birthday. Fergal's parents had planned a big day out for their young guests: a trip to Woodwind holiday park, there would be a treasure hunt among other activities, and there was to be a barbeque to round it all off.

Millie knew the mother from school. 'It will be fairly late, by the time we're finished,' she had told Millie. 'We'll drop the children home, of course.'

Millie pulled her overcoat more closely around her. It really was cold and getting colder by the minute. As every year, she had bought presents for Mad Bobby and Jimbo as well as for the children. Now that Sherry was running Mrs Foley's shop and Jessica driving the twins to and from school, she had been able to take on two extra cleaning jobs which meant she could buy a few extra treats for everyone this year. She ran over in her head the list of things she had planned to buy today, hoping she had not forgotten something vital. With the weather like this and with Mrs Foley's shop closed for a few days, she did not relish the prospect of having to come back here for anything she needed.

She heard distant shouts and then three teenagers appeared, chasing each other down the street, laughing and shouting at the tops of their voices. One of them tripped over her shopping bags sending them flying, the contents scattered into the street. With a gasp of dismay, Millie scrambled to collect the packages, fearful that they would get run over by a passing car.

'Want a hand?'

The voice came from behind her as she bent down to retrieve the packages. Before she knew it, Jason DeVries was beside her helping to collect the scattered items.

Millie's heart did a somersault and started to race like a mad thing. She had no idea he had returned to the area.

His hand touched hers as he put the last package back into the shopping bag. 'You're freezing,' he said.

'I'm all right.' She had to fight to get the words out, her heart was beating somewhere up in her throat. 'Thank you', she managed to add.

'Let's get you warmed up. We can have a hot drink at the Corner Café and I'll drop you home afterwards. Are the kids here with you?'

'No, they're at a birthday party.' Her voice still sounded wobbly.

'Good.' He picked up her two shopping bags and piloted her to the The Corner Café, finding them seats facing each other at the back.

Millie was afraid to look at Jason, afraid he could read in her face how pleased she was to see him. Then common sense kicked in. No need to get over-excited. He was just being kind. She did need to thank him, though, for what he had done and was doing for Mrs Foley even if he had not wanted it mentioned.

He ordered hot chocolate for both of them then turned his attention to her, trying to get her to look directly at him.

'How have you been, Millie? Maybe you're wondering why I'm here. I hope you are.'

When she did not say anything, he went on. 'I had to come back. Had to try one more time.' He leaned towards her across the table. 'Look at me, Millie. You know I said I wouldn't come on to you but I have to give it a shot. I sort of thought you liked me, a little bit anyway. Stop me, if you don't want to hear me out.'

She looked at him then, her heart too full to say a word.

'That's a yes?'

She nodded, half afraid she would wake up from the happiest of dreams.

'I couldn't stop thinking about you, Millie. I know this isn't the right moment. I should be on my knees with a bunch of roses in the moonlight. It's not very romantic, is it, drinking hot chocolate in the Corner Café in Greenfields? On the other hand, the last time I wanted to tell you how I feel, you turned your nose up at me like I was something Mrs Foley's cat left on the best rug.'

That made her laugh. 'I didn't think you cared about me anyway.'

'I wanted to show you that I wasn't really that bad but every time I thought I was making progress, you turned away from me. And then on that night up at Fernwood House when I explained to everyone that you could all stay as tenants and nothing would change, I sort of hoped you'd come up to me afterwards but you wouldn't look at me and then you just disappeared. I nearly gave up then, to be honest.'

'I'm sorry. I thought you were just being kind because you felt sort of guilty about turfing us out. And then I kept asking myself what you'd see in me anyway.'

'What I'd see in you?' He repeated. 'I can tell you that I saw someone who cared deeply about other people. I had never really met someone like that before I met you.'

He leaned across the table and kissed her full on the lips, upsetting the milk jug in the process.

Fortunately, the waitress appeared with their hot chocolate at the same moment. During the pause which followed as the spilled milk was being mopped up and the table given a rub down by the waitress, Millie had time to pull herself together as best she could. The touch of his lips on hers had melted her bones, her heart felt as if it would escape her ribcage for sheer joy.

'I wanted to hate you,' she said slowly, her voice sounding breathless to her own ears. 'You were throwing us out of our cottages and I was really angry at you. I didn't want to like you.'

He held up a hand. 'Let's forget all that. I am so grateful for the lessons I learned from everyone at Fernwood Cottages. But I'm more than grateful that I met you, Millie.'

'There's one thing I have to mention,' she said. 'Thank you so much for what you did and are doing for Mrs Foley. She told me not to mention it but I just have to say it. That is so kind of you. And I think you're funding this mini holiday for her and her sister now, too, aren't you?'

'Let's leave Mrs Foley out of it,' he said with a laugh. 'I did it all for you, you were so worried about her.'

They sat, holding hands across the table and he told her how much she meant to him. And of course they both tried to remember exactly when the attraction started.

'I think it was when Mrs Foley had her accident,' Jason said. 'There you were, standing in the dark and soaking wet guarding Mrs Foley like a lioness.'

'Sounds very romantic,' Millie laughed.

'What about you? When did you stop hating me?' He wanted to know.

''I'm not sure,' she confessed. 'You told me I was trespassing when I first met you, and then you were so kind and helpful especially to Maeve and Danny, and yet I couldn't forget that you were evicting us all. I really fought it but when you went away and didn't come back for Mrs Foley's party, I realized how much I cared about you.'

'Like missing a noise when it stops? That sounds equally romantic, so we're quits. In fact I had a bit of negotiating to get through about the house and my decision to leave everything as it is. There were a lot of things I needed to clear up. I kind of liked the house for itself but I knew I could never live there if you weren't by my side, Millie. I had to come back and try one more time to see if you really hated me.'

He kissed her again across the table, being careful not to upset the milk jug this time.

'I want to kiss you properly,' he told her, 'without an audience. Let's go home.'

Millie looked at her watch. 'Is that the time?. The children will be back from their party soon and I need to hide their presents until Christmas morning.' She smiled at him. 'They'll be so pleased to see you again.'

'And I'll be pleased to see them.'

They walked to his car, hand in hand with the first white flakes of snow starting to fall in earnest.

Maeve and Danny were indeed ecstatic at the sight of Jason. They took it serenely for granted that he was seated on the shabby couch in front of the fire in the kitchen when they returned from their party. They ran to him and he enveloped them in a big hug.

'Will you be here for Christmas?' Maeve asked shyly.

He smiled down at her. 'I certainly hope so.'

'Can we play in the yard at Fernwood House again?' This from Danny.

'Most definitely.' Jason told him with half a glance at Millie.

Millie had never seen him so happy. Why had she ever thought he was dark and brooding? When he looked at her, she felt her insides melt from sheer happiness.

'Is Jason going to be our new daddy?' Danny asked later when they were all seated round the fire. The twins had been looking from one to the other of them, highly sensitive to the emotional cross-currents between grown-ups as children usually are.

Jason raised an eyebrow at her before turning to the little boy. 'It would be nice, wouldn't it?' He looked at Millie who was seated close beside him. 'What do you say? Will you marry me?'

'Yes,' the children chorused.

Millie laughed. 'Then I say yes. Yes to all three of you'.

And so they made their vows to each other, sitting in the shabby little kitchen while the children bounced up and down with delight.

'It's going to be the best Christmas ever,' they chanted.

****

Made in the USA
Middletown, DE
29 November 2025